R1

HELEN McCOURT MENTEK

TRAFFORD PUBLISHING

Victoria, Canada
New Bern, U.S.A
Crewe, U.K.
Drogheda, Ireland
Madrid, Spain

© Copyright 2004 Helen McCourt Mentek. All rights reserved.

No part of this publication may be reproduced, stored in a retrieval system, or transmitted, in any form or by any means, electronic, mechanical, photocopying, recording, or otherwise, without the written prior permission of the author.

Printed in Victoria, Canada

A cataloguing record for this book that includes the U.S. Library of Congress Classification number, the Library of Congress Call number and the Dewey Decimal cataloguing code is available from the National Library of Canada. The complete cataloguing record can be obtained from the National Library's online database at: www.nlc-bnc.ca/amicus/index-e.html
ISBN: 1-4120-1902-8

TRAFFORD

This book was published *on-demand* in cooperation with Trafford Publishing. On-demand publishing is a unique process and service of making a book available for retail sale to the public taking advantage of on-demand manufacturing and Internet marketing. **On-demand publishing** includes promotions, retail sales, manufacturing, order fulfilment, accounting and collecting royalties on behalf of the author.

Suite 6E, 2333 Government St., Victoria, B.C. V8T 4P4, CANADA
Phone   250-383-6864   Toll-free   1-888-232-4444 (Canada & US)
Fax   250-383-6804   E-mail   sales@trafford.com
Web site www.trafford.com   TRAFFORD PUBLISHING IS A DIVISION OF TRAFFORD HOLDINGS LTD.
Trafford Catalogue #03-2280   www.trafford.com/robots/03-2280.html

10   9   8   7   6   5

Introduction

Like many children growing up in a small community, I was imaginative and curious about the lives of the people around me. And so it was that I became somewhat of a snoop - all eyes and ears - listening at open doors and peeking through windows. After all what else was there for a young girl to do in a tiny village?

You might think that village life was too dull and dry for stories to grow. But the joys and sorrows of villagers' lives are food for tales and gossip. Whether filled with optimism or inconceivable tragedy, these stories ebbed and flowed through the village like ripples on a puddle.

Some stories are centered around actual events, others are purely products of my imagination. The names of all of the characters depicted in this book have been changed, and no reference to persons living or dead is intended.

An old broom knows the dirty corners best - Irish Proverb

CONTENTS

Tamarack..1

The Medicine Show..12

The Sugar Shack and Other Calamities....................26

Beth's Folly 38

The Mourners..54

Three, Four, Shut the Door....................................63

The Perfect Lady...73

Dave's Brave New World......................................90

Paula's Journey...105

The Life of Granny Coombes..............................132

Web of Power...143

Escaping the Net...201

Under the Rose...214

The Wheel of Life...228

Bitter Herbs..265

ACKNOWLEDGMENTS

Avery Allisen   Cover Picture

Thanh Nguyen   Technical Adviser

Eileen Kraatz   Editor

My thanks to my husband, Ted, and my daughter, Kathleen Allisen, for their encouragement and support.

Tamarack

In 1869, the little village of Tamarack was founded by Sir William Caldwell, an Englishman who arrived in the village like Lord High Mucky-muck in his fancy garb. He was an official with the Northern Railway of Canada and had been called from England to oversee the operation of the fledgling railway. Sir William flung his weight around with a haughty voice that raised the hackles of the rough Colonials. The locals called him a "constipated stuck-up Limey." He would strut up and down the station platform bellowing orders and sneering down his red "pointy" nose at the toiling, sweat-stained section hands in their tattered overalls as they puffed on their corn-cob pipes and stunk up the air with cheap tobacco. Oh, they hated him all right! Folks still tell the most outrageous tales about him these many years later. Stories went the rounds of how he swindled the early settlers out of their lands and sold off his ill-gotten gains to the railway at fancy prices, pocketing the profits. People still talk of when he put one of the village girls in the family way, and then made a hasty retreat back to England. Those stories and other unflattering pictures of the vilified Sir William have remained part of village folklore for many years.

For as long as I can remember, our village of Tamarack was called a "town." It wasn't an official designation, as we were far too small for such a high-falutin' title. The little community was referred to as "uptown" or "downtown," depending on which end of it you lived. In either case it didn't take you long to get from one end to the other. "Uptown" consisted of five stores, a café and a hotel, all bordering the main street. It was the hub of commerce.

At the best of times there were only about five hundred souls living in the village. Some arrived out of nowhere and left just as mysteriously. No one knew where they came from or where they went. Nor did they care. The residents didn't take too kindly to their vagabond ways, and their departures were usually accompanied with sighs of relief and comments of "Thank God that bunch has finally cleared out." "Good riddance!" was often the cry ringing in their ears as they packed up their meagre belongings and moved on faster than a fart in the breeze!

Tamarack had always been a "dry town". After many tumultuous rows between the tipplers and the Christian League, who had the healthy support of the Society of the Daughters of Temperance, the stalwart Christian League won every battle hands down. The disgruntled losers nursed their defeats at the nearest beer parlour ten miles away or at one of the many "blind pigs" that dotted the countryside. But in the village you could only quench your parched throat with lemonade or a soft drink.

Our little dot of a village began as a pioneer settlement with a few ramshackle wooden buildings and two or three crude places of business clustered around the railway tracks. Sixty years later, the main street was just a short stretch of sidewalk on both sides of a main highway that sliced right through the middle of the village.

At one end of this strip, McCann's Groceries offered the usual variety of staples. You would never find any exotic prizes in the tidy store-cum-residence of the McCann's. The Mister, nicknamed Beau, appeared every day nattily dressed in his tan checkered suit and bowler hat and looking very much like a comic in a vaudeville act. If he'd had a diamond stickpin fastened to his tie, he would have been the picture of a prosperous country squire. Not to say he didn't have his eye on a sparkler only slightly smaller than his thumbnail, but he didn't own it yet. There was stiff opposition from his "missus" for such an extravagance. With his savoir-faire manner and grand appearance, Beau was a fine specimen of a rural gentleman. He was the wealthiest cattle buyer in the township. There wasn't a man in the village as well liked as Beau McCann. He was looked upon as an important, civic-minded person by the village folk, and his advice was regularly sought on all sorts of matters, personal as well as financial. He was the village "Oracle," pontificating in the local hotel on all sorts of topics from child-rearing to the country's economy.

The operation of the store was handled by his wife, Nicky, shortened from Veronica years ago by her baby sister who couldn't manage the whole name. Nicky was a stern, beanpole of a woman, who gave you short shrift if she caught you sneaking a few candies from her counter display.

At the other end of the main street, Emmett Miller's butcher shop stood in grimy silence, its heavy sign swaying and squeaking on rusty hinges, the faded red paint sliding off the rotting wood.

Emmett Miller's two sons, Ems, Jr. and Artie, were more of a hindrance than a help to the business. Their days were spent adrift in an alcoholic haze when they weren't dipping into the till to finance another drunken spree. In a few years, they'd managed to bankrupt the business. Their father was never able to figure out what had happened to his thriving butcher shop. Never blessed with a head for business, Emmett only knew how to cut meat.

Between these two commercial endeavours, the proprietors of several more aged structures managed to eke out a living. Family-owned and operated Lalonde's Hardware enjoyed a brisk business from the local farmers and the village people. There was always a need for hammers and nails and, later on, pots and pans and dishes. Being a shrewd businessman, Oscar knew that a need can become an opportunity if one seizes it, and he promptly added a variety of household goods to his inventory. He would greet you with a hearty "Bon Jour! Ca va?" as soon as the little bell tinkled above the door, even though he had yet to see your face. He always greeted his customers in French. But unless you were a part of the three French families in the village, conversations were carried on in English, in his heavy French accent. A friendly fellow, Oscar would flap around his customer like an agitated goose eager to help select just the right nail or screw from the bins that lined one wall of his store.

Across the road loomed the Tamarack Hotel, a three-story building of gray asphalt siding that towered over everything. Russell, Arnold and young Cornwallis, the three sons of the owner, Enoch Trotter, worked in the hotel with their father.

When Russell and Arnold were born in quick succession, Mrs. Trotter left the job of disciplining them to Enoch. But when his wife gave birth to another son a few years later, she immediately seized the baby and named him Cornwallis after she'd read an article about Sir Charles Cornwallis in the National Geographic. The long-dead Sir Charles had been a British General and Statesman, and the first Marquis of Cornwall. Maria Trotter thought Cornwallis was a splendid name for her son, a name that would recognize their "Britishness," of which she was extremely proud. She even had the absurd idea that he would cut a figure in the world. Some folks thought the Trotters were actually related to the Marquis, although where that gossip started nobody knew for sure. Mrs. Trotter did little to dispel the tale. It wasn't easy for the little boy to attend school every day with a name like Cornwallis. But his mother had insisted on it. Maria Trotter had always lived in a fantasy world that was far more grandiose than the real one she lived in. Little Cornwallis was stuck with the name and the endless taunts of his school-mates until his teens when he acquired the nick-name "Corny." For the rest of his life, he was just known as "Corny" and his real name was gradually forgotten.

The three Trotter brothers shared the duties at the reception desk and the snack bar just inside the heavy oak front door. Helping out with simple chores was fourteen-year-old Tommy Frawley. Tommy was taken into the Trotter household after the death of his parents and his four siblings from the Spanish flu epidemic in 1918. For some reason Enoch had made a death-bed promise to the widowed Ida Frawley as she lay gasping her last feverish breath. He'd promised to care for the boy.

Speculation persisted in the village as to the paternity of the lad, and why he ended up in the Trotter family. Some thought he was Enoch's love-child. Others scoffed at the very idea. The rumours about young Tommy and his dubious father were hotly denied by Enoch's friends, who refused to listen to such gossip. The secret, if there was one, remained buried with Tommy's mother.

The Trotters cared for Tommy all of his life until he died at the age of eighty-two. He was always considered a member of the family as much as Enoch considered any of the boys his family. Enoch was an autocratic father, an austere, stony-faced man who demanded total obedience from his wife and sons. He forbade the boys to hobnob with what he considered the village riff-raff. But, of course, they did anyway and suffered their punishments when their father found out. He insisted that his sons polish their boots every day before they left for school and that their shirt collars were clean and suitably starched. The boys were teased without mercy over their "sissy clothes." They hated to be all dressed up when many of their school friends had no shoes and barely enough clothing to cover their thin bodies.

Next door to the hotel, Oscar Lalonde's three daughters opened up a small dry goods store called "Colette's Specialty Shoppe," named after the oldest sister. Colette did all the buying of the bolts of material and clothes to fit the chic, as well as the mountainous shapes of her clientele. Every purchase went into a paper bag embossed with a sketch of the store and the slogan, "All Roads Lead to Colette's." The business was successful despite all the bickering and squabbling among the three sisters. At times, passing by the open door, you could hear them arguing in loud, high-pitched voices. "Mind your own business!" Colette would shout. "Just take care of the customers and don't meddle in things you don't understand. You never did have a lick of sense between the two of you!" This tirade would often happen when a cunning salesman would try to pawn off some unsaleable merchandise on the two gullible sisters. Colette's rebukes seldom went unanswered, and would result in tearful shrieks of "Bitch!" or "Cochon!" followed by a volley of French, that you just knew wasn't anything complimentary. If, by chance, a customer happened to come into the store in the middle of all the shouting, everything miraculously became all smiles and sugary sweetness.

  At the tail-end of this cluster of commerce, Benson's Garage and Taxi Service clung to an oily, cracked cement platform. The building itself was in desperate need of attention, as was its owner, Isadore Benson. Izzy, as he was known around the village, would often disappear in the middle of the night, clad only in his white nightshirt and rubber gumboots, carrying his saw and lantern, and heading for the cottages surrounding the lake. He would stop every few minutes and cock his head from side to side like a robin listening for worms. Sometimes he would lift his head and bellow at the sky. He moved about in the moonlight with his lantern like a wizened grim reaper, darting through the woods like a giant firefly. All night he would busy himself sawing whole trees and bushes that he said were a blight on the landscape. Izzy never thought he was a trespasser on private property. In his mind he was doing the cottage owners a favour. But there was one gentleman who didn't welcome Izzy's help.

Mr. Willson, from Toronto, spent his whole summer vacation at his cottage on the lake, erecting a spanking new outhouse, the "two-holer" kind with a half-moon cut-out high up on the door. He carefully painted his masterpiece in a deep forest green. Two coats he put on it so the colour would blend in with the green shrubbery and the spruce trees around it that concealed its presence from passers-by. But Mr. Willson hadn't heard of the "curse of the cottagers." No one knew where Izzy might strike next. One summer night, with unswerving tenacity, Izzy totally obliterated Mr. Willson's curtain of trees and shrubs, right down to their stumps. The following week-end, Mr. Willson drove up from Toronto to observe the fruits of his labour, only to be greeted by a lonely tower of green, adorned with a sign, "The Palace of Sighs," that he'd diligently painted in fancy white script. The new edifice stood out like a beacon for all to see.

Mr. Willson's angry comments could not be repeated in polite company.

Izzy's behaviour was looked upon with great amusement, and tolerated only out of sympathy for his wife. Libby Benson was a staunch member of the United Church. She generously devoted many hours to the doings of the local chapters of the Women's Institute and the Ladies' Aid. She was a God-fearing pillar of the community. As for Izzy's escapades, there were always some local men on hand to foray into the woods, scoop up the poor fellow and return him to his long-suffering wife.

On the corner where the highway curved over the railway tracks, a newly-arrived Chinese family opened up a small café. Mr. Wong had a struggle at first as the English and French townspeople weren't too open-minded about having a pigtailed foreigner in their midst. But with perseverance, the affable Mr. Wong produced an array of Oriental dishes that the villagers had never seen the likes of before. Egg-drop soup with tender little dumplings the size of quarters, chicken fried rice, and crispy brown egg rolls with a plum sauce like nectar from the gods. All was topped off with his special Oolong tea served in tiny white cups. It wasn't long before the scoffers began to flock to his café. As they feasted on Mr. Wong's delicacies, his hodgepodge of English and Chinese was the source of great entertainment for his patrons. On market day, he rallied his whole family together, all eight of the Wong children and Mrs. Wong, and the tiny café fairly vibrated with the clamour for food. Orders were yelled in rapid-fire Chinese to a frazzled Mrs. Wong, while she yelled back from the kitchen.

This was the nature of our village sixty years ago - a sparse group of buildings strung together like paper cutouts.

Today Tamarack carries the same neglected look. But they're all gone now. All the friends and neighbours I knew as a child have died or moved away. New families have put down roots in the village. The old houses are the same but the newcomers seem like intruders who couldn't care less about the past. When I stroll around the village and pass all those unfamiliar faces on the street, I can't help feeling resentful. Tamarack is a place to be born in, to live in and die in. Not for strangers.

The Medicine Show

Every fall, Tamarack was visited by a rag-tag group of amateur performers called "The Medicine Show." There was nothing special about the entertainers. They were just ordinary people striving to keep body and soul together in the desperate years of the "Dirty Thirties." If you were poor, and most people were then, and if you could sing and dance a little, or play any kind of a musical instrument, all the better. You could work the shows for your keep, and have a little pocket money to boot. There were always plenty of free-spirited drifters who couldn't resist the lure of the road. There was such a freedom to it! When you were off travelling around the little communities, there were no snooping wives or mothers breathing down your neck. Only the demands of the show's owner, and he didn't give a tinker's curse what you did in your spare time as long as you showed up sober and did your job.

The whole community looked forward to opening night. Weeks in advance, hand-printed notices were tacked up in the Post Office and on every post and pole for miles around. What a welcome reprieve it was from the eternal boredom of rural living! You had to make your own fun in those days and, for the most part, it was skating at the outdoor rink in winter or, if you were lucky enough to latch onto a pair of skis or snow-shoes, there were plenty of hills to test your mettle. After supper it was great fun to toboggan down the snow-covered hills until darkness forced us to go home.

In summer, our youth was idled away swimming in the nearby lake and building rafts from old barrels and boards to punt around the weedy creeks that seeped in from the lake over the low ground. Fishing was a favourite pastime and, in the early days of spring you could often see someone skulking along the highway with his illegal spear half hidden beneath his coat. A fresh pickerel or two, caught out of season, guaranteed a mouth-watering spread.

My thoughts drift back many years. It was early September. School had just begun. One sunny morning, Beth, my younger sister, and I left home for the two-room schoolhouse. We hurried to catch up with our friends ahead.

The Senior Room, where Beth and I were hostaged in Grades Five and Eight was already spilling over with excitement. Plans were being laid to convince our parents that the Medicine Show was a good thing, and we were desperate to go. The buzz in the room rose to a high pitch as we talked about "What Mom said" and "What Dad said" when we'd tried our parents' patience with our constant begging. We counted on the tried and true method of children of all generations: "If you can go, I can go." We thought if we could get two or three parents to consent, the rest would tumble like dominoes.

The noisy din was interrupted when our teacher, Miss Lavender, swept into the room and shot her bony arm into the air. "Quiet!" she bellowed. Her voice was like the crack of a whip across the room and had much the same effect. Her eyes were as hard and black as peppercorns and her toothpick body bristled with authority. A hush settled over the classroom. Miss Lavender's bird-like eyes roamed around the room as if on the lookout for anyone who might dare to even whisper. In those days the power of one teacher was never tested by any foolhardiness on the part of a student. The dreaded strap was always within easy reach of her long arms. And you'd get the same when you got home.

Some parents had concerns as to whether the upcoming show would be "clean and wholesome" for their young daughters. At that age, I couldn't imagine what an "unclean" show was. So I questioned my mother. "I don't know what you mean by 'clean and wholesome,' Mother," I said. "What's the matter with people singing and dancing or playing the guitar? Grandpa Coombes plays his guitar, and he's always clean," I reasoned. "And I've even seen him dancing around the kitchen with Grandma!"

Mother frowned in silence. If she was amused by that she didn't show it. "Well, Melissa," she began, "I think it might be too late at night for you and Beth. And you have school the next day, you know."

A doubtful "Oh" was all I said, as I puzzled over that for a few minutes. I wasn't convinced and thought she was hiding some important information from me. In those days mothers weren't too anxious to divulge any secrets of a sexual nature to their curious young daughters, fearing that too much knowledge could lead to checking things out for themselves. There had been times when some shows had been downright indecent.

Our parents did relent, secure in their belief that no one would dare to perform an "unclean" show on United Church property.

The church hall had been rented out to the performers by the Reverend Graves for $20, a sum that the good Reverend thought would make up for the absence of the members of the Burning Bush Prayer Group from their regular Monday night meeting. Some of the members had already appointed themselves as moral watchdogs and they would be feasting their eyes on the goings-on in the church hall instead of praying for their eternal salvation as was their custom on Monday nights.

By opening night, Beth and I and most of our school friends had been successful in our relentless campaigns at home. Bessie Clarke was going, Birdie McMahon was going and Carrie Gregg, whose mother was a no-nonsense Methodist, was given the OK.

A sober cluster of adults waited, watching our noisy behaviour with dark frowns. The men were dressed in ill-fitting Sunday suits, jackets straining at the underarms, their neckties tight around bulging red necks. The women, stout and work-worn and tightly corseted, huddled together like a flock of faded pigeons.

At last the hall door opened and the jostling crowd moved forward. Inside there were the scraping sounds of shifting chairs and a noisy scuffle began for the best seats. Cries of "Over here, Annie!" "Get out of my way!" and "Bugger off! I was here first!" rang out, filling the room with a deafening uproar.

And it was stifling hot inside. Steam hissed and boiled through the radiators producing a humid, overwhelming swelter. A rising odour of mildew mixed with the pungent smell of mothballs began to permeate the air, blending with whiffs of sour perspiration that hung over us like a fetid cloud.

When everyone had settled into their seats, a quiet descended. Major Winston, the Master of Ceremonies introduced himself and welcomed everyone to the show. He perched on the stool at the old upright piano, and stormed through a clanging rendition of "God Save the King." On cue everyone rose to their feet. The adults stood stiffly at attention in the old-fashioned way, when people wore their patriotism with pride. The youth around them whispered and giggled in restless anticipation.

As the final notes of the anthem reverberated throughout the hall, Major Winston scrambled up onto the stage, stepping so lightly one would think he wouldn't have broken eggs if they were under his feet. He was a low built, middle-aged, chunk of a man. White muttonchop whiskers framed his ruddy face. His white hair flew out from his scalp like a snowfall as he darted around the stage. He beamed and postured before the applauding audience as he wiped away the perspiration from his brow. His voice bonged across the room as he announced the first act of the show.

"'Ere she is, folks," he bellowed from the stage above us, gesturing toward the wings with one hand, the other braced against his hip. "Dodi Delaney, Cel-ee-brated Singer and Dancer - Fresh from the New York stage." Of course, she had never been within a donkey's roar of New York, or the Broadway stage, but we didn't know that, and our excitement grew as we waited for Dodi to appear.

All eyes strained toward the stage. A bare thigh appeared first from behind the curtained wings, and a roar went up from the crowd. The men in the audience winked and nudged each other as out onto the stage pranced a glittering spectacle in a red satin costume speckled with gold sequins. You couldn't say Dodi was beautiful, she wasn't even pretty. Her broad face was lathered with heavy make-up, and her pouty lips were sticky with crimson lipstick. Her long hair was caught up in an explosion of daffodil frizz. There was an air of show-biz splendour about Dodi that dazzled the crowd. She quavered through an off-key rendition of "Shine on Harvest Moon" with hand and body movements so disconnected she seemed like a puppet on strings. But she was no wooden doll when she began to tap dance, and she rattled her way across the stage with Major Winston obliging at the piano. What Dodi lacked in talent she made up for in enthusiasm. Flesh quivered and shook as she tapped out her routine. Her skimpy red shorts revealed her jiggling thighs, and the slippery bit of crimson satin on top barely concealed her breasts bouncing up and down like two melons. The men were spellbound and shifted forward in their seats, their eyes glued to the bobbing vision before them. The air was electric with tension as they waited for the law of gravity to fail and Dodi's ample bosom to pop out of the scrap of cloth entrusted to its safekeeping. Sweat glistened on foreheads and eyes bulged in anticipation. In the bleak lives of these labouring men, sex, even as a topic of conversation, was denied them, for they hadn't had much to speak of.

  At the close of her act, Dodi whirled around in a risky pirouette, arms flailing and feet smacking the creaking floorboards in a pounding frenzy. But the hoped-for calamity didn't happen, and her scanty covering held fast to her heaving bosom.

Whistles and cheers rolled across the room, as men yelled and pounded the floor with their heavy boots. Hoarse cries of "Dodi! Dodi!" and "More, more!" filled the air. But it was not to be. Dodi flung herself into the wings with a cheery wave as her swaying rump disappeared from sight. The old building creaked and groaned because the noise was so thunderous.

With a collective sigh the men settled back in their seats feeling cheated out of what might have been a sensational climax. On the other hand, the women-folk pursed their prunish lips and clacked their tongues, as Dodi wiggled out of sight.

The audience finally calmed down as entertainment was temporarily abandoned and commerce took over. Major Winston bounced onto the stage to pitch his product. His "Magic Elixir" was guaranteed to cure everything from diphtheria to diarrhea. It didn't have much of a healing effect on anything, but it could wreak havoc on slim pocketbooks.

The entertainers doubled as salespeople, and they scampered up and down the aisles, peddling the worthless syrup. The corked bottles clinked together in cardboard boxes that were slung from their necks with strips of colourful, braided cloth. At the same time Major Winston stood on the stage extolling the benefits of a spoonful a day.

"It's the latest development in medicine, folks. Recommended by hundreds of doctors. Try it, and you'll agree! I guarantee it!"

With vigorous persuasion, he shared his message with the hesitant audience. Many were lacking in hard cash, and what little they had wasn't always spent on "real" medicine, unless it was a matter of life and death, and even then, the spending of it was always carefully considered. Money had always been an important part of their lives because there was never much of it around. Magic Elixir's chances for success were slim, except for a few impulsive souls who were willing to try anything rather than lay out for a doctor.

Soon an uneasy murmuring rustled throughout the hall as impatience to get on with the show began to take hold.

We could hear the low vagrant sounds of an accordion. From the edge of the stage Major Winston's booming voice announced the source.

"Ladies and Gentlemen, please welcome my good friend, Gino Spazianni, The Heart-throb of Naples. Come on out and take a bow, Gino!"

The Major pointed toward the wings, and out onto the stage glided the gorgeous Gino. He couldn't have been more than nineteen or twenty. My friends and I were immediately smitten and we gawked at him open-mouthed. His wide-set, black eyes glinted in the light as they roamed over the crowd. A soft smile touched his full red lips. Would he notice us? A gigantic mother-of-pearl accordion hung with red and gold tassels was strapped to his body. He was a heart-throb in a smouldering, erotic way. His flashing fingers brought forth a rousing "Funiculi Funicula" as he rocked back and forth with a grin on his face that hovered between arrogance and sensuality. His black hair was pomaded flat against his skull and shone like a satin cap. Tight black trousers with gold glitter threads hugged his body like a second skin. A white shirt, unbuttoned to expose a mat of black hair, kept the ladies a-twitter as they drank in his magnetism like thirsty cows. His long sleeves billowed out like white balloons as his fingers flew over the keys. A crimson cummerbund circled his waist. What a glorious contrast he was to the drab audience!

Gino never paused as he tore into a rendition of "Tarantella," followed by a quick medley of Italian folk tunes. All the while, he seduced his audience with the tempo of his music and his boyish grin. The highlight of his performance came as he tenderly caressed the keys, and in a velvety tenor crooned the words to "O Sole Mio" in such seductive and haunting tones that he had the audience dabbing at their eyes and blowing their noses with loud honking sounds. He completely captured the hearts of the women, and judging from their wistful expressions, caused some unsettling stirrings as his husky voice dredged up simmering desires that they'd buried long ago. Even the hardened men couldn't hold back their feelings, and they swiped at their leathery faces with clenched fists, so as not to be too obvious. It was likely their tears flowed from desperate hopes and fears, and the crushing poverty that had gripped their lives. Gino concluded his performance with a thundering "Granada," but the rousing music did little to curb the raw feelings of the crowd.

Silence followed Gino as he left the stage. For a few minutes everyone sat spellbound. Then suddenly the room erupted with the noise of clattering chairs. Some of the women tossed aside their dignity like an old boot, and rose to their feet, clapping in a loud rhythmic beat. Soon everyone joined in and kept it up. But the Latin charmer didn't return to the stage. A hoped for encore was nipped in the bud by the time-conscious Major, who saw to it that nothing stood in the way of legitimate commerce.

There was more scurrying up and down the aisles with Magic Elixir bottles rattling, as the little Master of Ceremonies trumpeted his sales pitch from the stage.

His shouts rang from the rafters as he harangued his audience. He waved a pointing finger over the room, singling out an unfortunate fellow in the front row.

"You, sir," he shouted at the startled spectator, "there in the front row. Are you troubled by sleepless nights after a long, hard day in the fields? Do you suffer cramps from what could be hungry little worms feasting in your belly? Would you like to be rid of those green globs you've been coughing up for years?" His finger jabbed the air. "The answer's 'ere, folks." He held up a bottle of the milky fluid. "My Magic Elixir!" he shouted, waving the bottle in the air. "Don't delay! They're going like hot cakes!" No one budged.

"C'mon, good people, last chance. Just 50 cents the bottle. Cheap at the price!" he implored.

But they couldn't dig any deeper, forcing Major Winston to abandon his enterprise. With three sharp whistles he summoned his trio of peddlers to the stage. They staggered back exhausted to finish the show. Time was running out and they had to pack up and be out by 11:00 o'clock. Quiet drifted over the crowd as Major Winston announced the last act.

"Our final performance this evening, folks, is by our own Paddy O'Leary, famous from across the seas and around the world for his unequalled talents on the banjo. He will warm your hearts with his fine Irish tenor. And here he is...Mister Paddy O'Leary!"

Paddy skipped onto the stage with a big smile and a jaunty salute to the cheering crowd. He was a bandy-legged, scraggy little man with wiry, orange-red hair. It sprang out from his skull as if electrified. He had the comic look of a goblin. He stepped lightly onto the stage, his feet barely touching the floor as he thrummed out a series of chords on his banjo.

A thunderous welcome greeted him with stomping and shouts that rose to the rafters. Paddy began to play and sing. The audience was silent as they listened to his rousing sounds of "The Rocky Road to Dublin." But soon they were clapping along to the rollicking tunes of "Whiskey in the Jar" and "The Wind That Shook the Barley." Paddy topped off his medleys with more reels and jigs and there was a great deal of clapping and foot banging from the audience. All the time, Paddy hopped from one foot to the other like a gleeful leprechaun, never missing a beat.

His fine tenor voice soared over the crowd as he sweetly embraced the lyrics of "My Wild Irish Rose." It was his grand finale.

With the last chord fading, an explosion of hoarse cries shook the old building. Major Winston scrambled onto the stage to silence the crowd. Dust filtered down as he concluded the show and thanked everyone for the good turn-out. He promised to return next year with an even bigger and better show. His little band of performers stood beside him with wide smiles, bowing to the shouts of approval from the audience.

Then began a frantic rush for the exit. People stumbled over each other in a mad struggle to escape the heat and breathe in the cool night air. Beth and I strolled down the street with our friends, arms linked. Our shrill laughter and girlish screams over the handsome Gino pierced the quiet of the evening. We fell silent as an old school bus rolled by, garishly painted in red letters six inches high spelling out "MAJOR WINSTON'S SHOW OF SHOWS."

The little Major gripped the wheel, his features set in a determined scowl as he headed for the next town and the next show. Weary faces stared out of the smudged windows, heedless of our frenzied efforts for their attention. We yelled and flapped our arms, but that dreamboat Gino didn't give us so much as a glance!

The Sugar Shack and Other Calamities

After breakfast, June and I tidied up the kitchen as Ken, her husband and my cousin, left for his job at the power plant. We always called him Nipper when we were children but nobody calls him that now unless it's just to tease him.

"I think I'll take a walk through the woods this morning, June," I said. "Do you want to come along?"

"Thanks, Melissa, but I'd better spend some time in the garden. I want to clear away some of the dead growth before it's time to plant. But you go ahead. Just don't go too far," she cautions. "It's become a jungle in there since you'd remember it."

I pulled on Ken's old mackinaw hanging on a peg behind the kitchen door and donned a pair of June's rubber boots.

"Enjoy yourself," she called out after me as I stepped outside.

The sun was bright and warm but it was still a cool spring morning. I paused outside and breathed deeply, filling my city lungs with the exhilarating air. As I hurried along the rough path I could smell the familiar, heady perfume of the woods - the scent of the moist earth, the grass and pine trees, and the sweetness of the Lily of the Valley peeping out from under blankets of dead leaves. The surroundings were a balm to my tired body. These woods have always stirred up fond memories, and that morning I was reminded of some childhood experiences that I'd almost forgotten.

Fifty years ago in the early spring, my young cousins would tap the big maple trees in the woods behind their house. Frank, Bill and the youngest, Kenneth lived with their parents in Rumbling Rapids, a remote community in northern Ontario. Their father, my Uncle Ben, was the superintendent of a large power plant on the Osseo River about thirty miles from Tamarack where I lived with my parents and my sister Beth.

When we were young girls, Beth and I looked forward to spending school holidays at Rumbling Rapids. Our cousins always had some misguided schemes going on either singly or together, depending on their compatibility at the time. Some of their projects turned out to be disasters. Like the time Frank and Bill built a tree house in the woods. It was to be a secret hideaway where they could smoke cigarettes stolen from their father's humidor and ogle the pictures of bare-breasted African women in the National Geographic. Poring over their father's magazines was the pornography of the day for young boys.

In their haste to build the tree house they hadn't solidly anchored the platform in the branches. Nipper was the first to go up to the "crow's-nest," spurred on by his older brothers, who generously gave him the honour of christening the wobbly structure with a bottle of red cream soda. It was just a ruse to see if the thing was safe. It wasn't. Nipper clutched the bottle of pop in one hand and struggled up the rickety ladder. As soon as he stepped onto the platform, the shaky contraption tipped over and threw him to the ground. His screams echoed through the woods. Frank and Bill tried to quiet him, holding their hands over his mouth and yelling at him to shut up. But they knew they would have to take him home where there'd be the devil to pay about it.

"What on earth have you two been up to?" Aunt DeeDee yelled. Nipper was standing in front of his mother, sobbing and cradling his arm.

"How did this happen? I want an explanation from the pair of you!" She pinpointed Frank and Bill with angry eyes.

"He... He fell out of a tree," Frank said.

"We told him not to go up there!" Bill lied.

"We'll just see about that," she yelled. "Go over to the power plant and get your father. We'll have to take him into Tamarack to Dr. Mills. I think his arm is broken!"

Ben sat in his office at the power plant as Bill and Frank stood stiffly in front of him and blurted out their version of the calamity. Ben guessed there was more to it than what his sons were telling him. He would get to the bottom of that later. He looked at his watch. They could still catch the afternoon train if they left right away.

The trip to Tamarack and Dr. Mills' office called for an hour's boat ride up the river and another forty-five minutes by train to Tamarack with Nipper whimpering in pain and his mother trying to comfort him. Bill and Frank kept their distance in silence.

After Dr. Mills had patched up Nipper with a cast, the family stayed at our house for the night and took the train home the next day. Beth and I went along to help. Frank and Bill kept to themselves, avoiding their father's stony glances.

The memory of it all floods back as I stand here in this cathedral of nature looking up at the tree. A few crumbling old boards still remain in the branches.

How moist and cool the soft dark moss is, screened by a canopy of leaves. As I walk along, the spongy carpet holds my footprints for a moment only to abruptly disappear as though I had never been there. The silence that surrounds me is invaded only by a few gossipy birds, some hungry robins and a flock of noisy crows. I can hear a woodpecker tapping somewhere on a dead tree. The sound echoes and re-echoes in the stillness.

~~

When we were all young and growing up together and when Beth and I were spending a few days with them, the boys always included us in their plans.

I smile as I remember the day Nipper returned home with the shiny new cast on his arm. Frank and Bill were unfazed by Nipper's injury. It didn't interfere with their plans and they went back to building the tree house. They finally succeeded in anchoring the platform between the branches. Nipper watched from below, relishing the prestige his snowy cast gave him. Its sparkling whiteness gave him a scrubbed look that was completely foreign to his usual grubby appearance. The attention and sympathy he was getting from his parents gave him an air of arrogance he would soon regret.

"Youse guys are doin' a bum job and you ain't never gonna finish it," he taunted from below, noisily sucking on a lollipop.

"And I hope yez both fall down and get dead!"

"Aw, shut up, you little baby," Frank roared back. "You ain't comin' up here when it's done, ya know, because ya never helped build it and you're just a little shit anyway!" Bill was clinging precariously to a tree branch as he hammered nails into the platform.

Nipper's bottom lip trembled. "Awww," he whined stretching out the sound like a rubber band. He was just ten. His older brothers never let him forget their authority. Bill saw Nipper struggling to hold back his tears.

"Cry Baby! Cry baby!" he sang out. Frank took up the chant.

"It ain't my fault! Youse done it! Youse broke my arm!" Sobbing, Nipper stumbled home where he got some sympathy from his mother.

It wasn't long after when Frank and Bill finally finished building the tree house that their father was taking a stroll to the edge of the woods after supper one evening. He noticed smoke billowing out from the tree-house. He raced back home and filled a pail with water. When he reached the tree he flung the water up into it. Seconds later, Frank's and Bill's drenched bodies crept out from under the dripping branches. They peered down at their father, eyes wide with alarm.

"What are you two doing up there?" Ben demanded.

"Nothing," they chorused and hung their heads.

"Don't tell me 'nothing'" he roared at them. "You were smoking up there, weren't you? After I told you how dangerous that is!" Guilt was written all over them.

"Get rid of it," Ben ordered jerking his head toward the tree house. For the next two days Frank and Bill laboured ripping out boards, swearing and heaving them to the ground. Nipper always denied it, but his brothers were sure he'd been tattling on them. That was the end of their little hide-away in the trees.

~~

I've come up to a grove of maples. I feel sure these are the same trees Nipper used to tap for syrup many years ago. I remember watching him drive the spigots into the tree trunks and hang little pails to catch the sap, always waiting for a bountiful yield.

We were both about fourteen one particular Easter holiday that I spent at Rumbling Rapids. The memory of it still haunts me and keeps me standing there gazing up at the old trees.

I can still feel the bite in the air that Saturday morning when Nipper and I left to check the sap pails. We left the gravel road at the edge of the woods and picked our way along the muddy path into the woods, shouting and laughing and pushing each other off the path. Our rubber boots squeezed bubbles of water from the wet leaves under our feet. Patches of snow lay on the ground. I stopped to pick the trilliums and violets peeking out from under the dead underbrush, always a sign that spring was on its way.

Nipper turned around to see what was keeping me. "C'mon, Melissa. The pails will be spilling over if we don't hurry up!" he yelled over his shoulder. I ran to catch up, afraid if he left me behind I would never find my way out of this bush and back to the house.

We walked on until we saw a ramshackle building looming ahead of us. The door was hanging by one hinge. The boys had found it abandoned one summer, and they immediately claimed it as the headquarters for their tree-tapping enterprise.

As we walked through the doorway, I stopped short, stunned. The walls of the old building were hung with a dozen or so gleaming white skulls. The floor was littered with shiny old bones. I was fascinated and at the same time repelled by the grisly sight. Empty eye sockets stared down like chaperones. A stale, cold smell of mould hung in the air.

"Nipper!" I whispered, grabbing him by the arm. "What is this spooky place? I'm not staying in here! C'mon! Let's go!"

"Oh, don't let a few old bones scare you, Melissa!" he laughed. "They ain't human, you know! This used to be a slaughterhouse. Some farmers did their butchering in here. These old skulls have been here for ages." He giggled. "Sometimes I bring city kids here when they're up at their cottages. It scares the shit out of them!" He laughed, braying like a donkey.

"C'mon over here!" he called out. "This is where I keep my pails and stuff." He pointed to a shelf that ran along one wall. It was encrusted with years of dirt and stained with black flaky patches of suspicious origin. I could see Nipper revelled in the sinister look of the old place. It was a real "House of Horrors" where imaginations could soar while he and his brothers waited for the sap to boil.

"No time to waste," he proclaimed with authority, as he slung a sack off his shoulder and dumped out some kindling and newspapers that he had brought with him.

"Get some rocks from over there," he ordered, nodding his head toward a pile beneath the trees. "Bigger!" he shouted when he saw the little stones I was picking up. When I'd gathered enough, Nipper sank to his knees and arranged them in a small circle. He tucked in the paper and kindling and struck a match. The wood smoldered as the groping flames licked around the paper. We stood for a few minutes warming our hands. Smoke spiralled up through the tall pine trees.

Once the fire had gained strength, Nipper went into the building and collected a pail from the shelf and an old blackened iron kettle. He stuck the end of an angle iron into the soft earth to hold the pot over the fire.

"I'll go empty the sap pails. You stay and watch the fire till I get back. Don't let it go out. And get some snow and wash out the pot," he yelled back at me. He stomped off self-importantly, whistling and tossing his pail into the air and was soon out of sight.

It wasn't long before I started to feel uneasy at being left alone in a place I knew nothing about. But I didn't want to complain since I had begged to come with him.

I gathered handfuls of snow and dropped them into the kettle. I found an old rag inside the building and swished it around with the snow in the kettle. It wasn't very clean but it would have to do. I poked at the fire adding a few bits of wood to keep it alive. I wished Nipper would get back.

Suppose he fell down and broke his leg or something, and nobody could find us? Squatting before the fire I dismissed those thoughts at once.

Suddenly I heard a movement in front of me. The rustling of dry leaves.

"Is that you, Nipper?" There was no answer. My heart thumping wildly, I slowly turned my head toward the sound. A small round head emerged from the leaves and swung around to face me. Its grey length began slowly undulating inch by inch toward me. Its mouth opened wide showing the soft pink inside and two bared fangs hiding a venom that would kill you in minutes. Its forked tongue licked the air. It was then that I heard the rattle and instantly recognized it. I'd heard it last summer here at Nipper's house. A Massassauga rattler had taken refuge under the verandah and was disturbed by the dog's frantic barking. Nipper had grabbed a shovel and, as the snake ventured out into the open, he chopped it in half right before my eyes. The sight of that had made me feel sick.

I remembered all this as I crouched paralyzed with fear by the dying fire for what seemed like hours.

My legs had become numb and I was desperate to stand up and get the circulation going. The snake had stopped moving and had coiled itself ready to spring. I squeezed my eyes shut expecting the worst. Nothing stirred. After a few minutes I opened one eye. The snake had turned its attention to something else. With a tremendous wave of something more than relief, I very carefully released my breath making no sound. I saw Nipper standing a few feet in front of me holding a thick tree branch. He placed his finger to his lips warning me to keep still as he crept softly toward the hesitating snake.

Whack! He slammed the branch down on the creature's coiled shape.

Whack! Whack! Again and again Nipper brought the branch down, slashing at the snake's writhing body. Blood spurted out, darkening its leafy bed. With it's head nearly severed and in its death throes I watched in a kind of a sickening fascination until there was no movement from it. I turned my head away as Nipper picked it up on the end of a stick and flung it into the woods.

By this time my legs were so numb I was too weak to stand up. When I tried, I tumbled over into the dirt. I didn't want to cry but tears came pouring down my cheeks. I rubbed my stiffened legs with one hand and wiped my eyes with the other. Nipper did his clumsy best to console me. He stamped out the fire, and threw handfuls of snow over it making sure it was out. We left everything where it was and hurried out of the woods away from that scene of terror. I was sobbing and unable to speak until we reached the house.

~~

All of these memories wash over me as today I stand in the cool dampness of the woods. Suddenly I hear a rustling of dead leaves. The noise jerks me out of my reverie. Thoughts of the snake are still in my mind. I whirl around and there behind me is Ken rustling the leaves with a stick and grinning like a circus clown.

"What did you think?" he chortles. "Another rattler?" His booming laughter echoes through the quiet woods.

"You never change do you, Nipper!" I put my arm around him and we leave the woods and our childhood behind.

Beth's Folly

We were gathered on the veranda after supper one warm summer night with my parents and Uncle Charlie and Aunt Mary. My two young cousins, Tim and Peter, were squabbling and shoving each other as young boys often do in playful camaraderie.

It was all in darkness, except for the flare of my father's cigar, that alternately glowed and receded in the darkness, and a timid flame of a citronella candle on the wicker porch table to drive away the annoying night insects. The only sounds were the squeaking of the wicker chair as my mother rocked back and forth with my five-year old sister, Beth, asleep on her lap while a mosquito whined over her head.

I don't remember how old I was. I think about ten or so, but I know I was old enough to realize that between the life of adults and the life of children, there's a wide gap that's rarely crossed by a child. And so, I sat quietly on the steps in the dark, hugging my bare knees and listening to the soft voices weaving through the quiet night air. It was my nature to be an eavesdropper, and I was taking in every word of gossip that flowed among the adults.

The air was perfumed with the scent of honeysuckle climbing on the trellises. My father's cigar glowed brighter, a signal that he was gearing up for one of his famous stories.

"Did I ever tell you the one about the fellow in the nudist colony?" He spoke to no one in particular and didn't expect an answer. He was going to tell it anyway. There were giggles from the children, for it was likely the first time they'd heard it. Mother glanced at my Aunt Mary and clacked her tongue in protest. She was already familiar with most of his repertoire. Uncle Charlie winked encouragingly at my father and he pressed on undaunted. His voice was low and confidential as he plunged into his story.

"Well, there was this young man checking out a nudist camp, you see, with an eye to joining up. As he looked around everything seemed to be in order, except for one old codger leaning against a tree. The young man couldn't help but notice that the wizened fellow was sporting a long gray beard. Down to his knees it was. Except for this luxuriant growth, the rest of him was buck-naked. This piqued the lad's curiosity and he went up to him and questioned him.

'Excuse me, sir,' he said, peering down at him, for the lad was about a foot taller. 'How come you're the only man in this here camp sportin' a beard? And why in blue blazes have you grown it so long?'

The knobby-kneed little chap thought for a minute, scratched his head and looking the young lad straight in the eye, drawled, 'Well, it's like this, sonny, someone has to go for coffee!'"

Everyone laughed even though most had heard it before. My father leaned back in his chair, folded his hands over his ample belly, and gave a strong pull on his cigar lighting up his twinkling eyes.

When all was quiet again Beth settled back drowsily in Mother's arms. Then Uncle Charlie remembered a relative who was sick or in trouble, and this would lead to the "who is married to who" puzzle, and "what was his wife's mother's name?" And on and on in endless discussions, each sharing a bit of family news that must never be repeated to outsiders. This is how the children learned about their world from offhand comments and family gossip and how all this assortment of relatives and friends fits into the tapestry of their lives.

Life was simple back then until the war began in September of 1939 and held us in its terrible grip for six long years. Many young men and women from Tamarack joined the armed forces. When the hostilities finally came to an end in 1945, some came home, and some did not. Cousin Tim, who was swatting flies and punching Peter his younger brother on our porch that night so long ago, had his life cut short at Dieppe. He was only twenty-two. Later we learned that Tim had never even set foot in France. He was hit by an enemy barrage as he jumped from the landing craft into the water in an attempt to reach the beach. He died alone in an angry, reddening sea. He wasn't even in the fight.

The day the news came, Uncle Charlie, who was the stationmaster at the time, received the message on the teletype. It began with the usual - "We regret to inform you…" Somehow, he managed to get home and deliver the terrible news to Aunt Mary. It was a blow that could have ripped them apart, but they clung together, the strength of their love carrying them through the long months and years that followed. Nothing would ever be the same for them again.

Because of his young age, Peter served only a short stint in the Royal Canadian Air Force. The war ended before he got into it. He was only eighteen and to his parents great relief, he'd spent all of his flying career in Canada. But Pete was haunted by that. He'd had some idea of avenging his brother's death, and when the war ended he'd returned to civilian life feeling restless and unfulfilled. After months of soul-searching, he entered the seminary. Today he is a missionary living in Zimbabwe, Africa. He serves out of a small mission on the edge of the capital of Harare. Father Pete has dedicated his life to saving souls in a country that seems indifferent to the plight of its own citizens. When he visits me, which is pretty much a yearly event now, his stories have replaced my father's, although Father Pete's are true, and often not so humorous.

Many years have passed, and as I look back on our lives, I feel sad that the comfortable intimacy of our families has passed away. Not only because of the distances we have placed between ourselves in miles and relationships, but also the deaths and the other changes in our lives. My parents, Uncle Charlie and Aunt Mary are all gone now and also poor Tim who left us so young.

But I'm getting away from my story about my young sister Beth, and her impetuous leap to independence at a sheltered age of eighteen. Beth told me this story as we sat talking together on my verandah many years later. She told it with a far-away look in her eyes, and with sudden bursts of laughter as she recalled the escapades of her youth.

The year she graduated from high school, 1943 it was, she took a summer job as a waitress at Wilderness Lodge to help with college expenses in the fall. That was the plan our parents had agreed to. But Beth had a plan of her own, and that was to have a good time and to be free to do as she pleased for the next two months, away from the watchful eyes of our parents.

There were several other young people working at Wilderness Lodge that summer. Johnny and Hank had been hired on as busboys. They, too, were trying to put aside some money for college. Along with Beth, there was one other waitress, Vera, whose family lived on a farm about five miles down the road. She seemed to have the freedom that Beth coveted.

"She's a little wild, but she's not a bad girl," her parents would say to anyone who might feel obliged to tell them of their daughter's latest harebrained scheme gone wrong.

Vera's loud voice and "don't give a damn" attitude was an invisible hook to the naive Beth. It was Vera who held the key to a fun-filled summer, and with blinkers in place, Beth was ready for a little action.

There was the night when after they'd finished their kitchen chores, Vera talked Beth into hitchhiking into the nearby town. Nothing of interest was happening around the lodge. Johnny and Hank had gone out fishing with some of the guests, so the girls decided to check out some of the local hangouts and have some fun. After spending several hours dancing at a roadhouse on the edge of town, they accepted a ride back to the lodge with two local fellows who had cozied up to them in the tavern. Vera began badgering the driver right away to let her drive, and he foolishly gave in when she assured him that she had a driver's permit and knew how to handle a car.

"After all," she said, "I drive my dad's tractor and his Chrysler all the time, so how hard can your old jalopy be?"

It was all a lie. Her father wouldn't let her within ten feet of his tractor and as for his car, well, "In a pig's eye!" he would roar whenever she asked to take it for a spin. He drove it himself only to go to church on Sundays and for weekly shopping trips into town with her mother. All Vera knew about the mechanics of driving was the accelerator, and that night she tromped down on it hard, sending the car whizzing down the road in a shower of gravel.

She began to bellow "Come Josephine in My Flying Machine," at the top of her lungs and paid no attention at all to the curve in the road ahead. Luckily, there was no traffic at that late hour. When she took her eyes off the road to argue with the owner who was screaming at her to slow down, she hit the ditch with a loud thump. The car teetered and rolled onto the passenger side. There was a jumble of arms and legs as the four occupants landed on top of one another. For a minute there was only a deathly silence. Then Vera scrambled up, jerked open the door and clambered out.

"C'mon, kiddo," she yelled at Beth. "Let's get the hell out of here!"

Beth climbed over the seat and together they sprinted through the woods, stumbling over tree roots and rocks. They arrived at the lodge out of breath and exhausted.

Back at the accident scene, the boys were fuming and cursing Vera. They were left to deal with the tow-truck and the police who had been called by a man who saw it all from the verandah of his cottage. No one suspected the girls' involvement.

Today as we sat together on my porch, we laughed at such outrageous antics. Then Beth remembered something else.

One night she and Vera were thumbing to a dance at Pine-Acres Resort on the other side of the lake. There was little traffic on the road and they were about to give up and turn back to the Lodge, when a car of ancient vintage rolled by and stopped. The driver backed up to where the girls were standing by the side of the road. He leaned out of the open window and shouted, "Want a lift, girls? Hop in." He jerked his thumb toward the back seat. Vera jumped in with no hesitation. Beth looked inside the open door. An odd looking fellow sat in the passenger seat. His hair was a straggly dirty blonde. He stared at her with a vacant look. His fat body was slumped in the seat. She hesitated. She didn't like the look of either of them, particularly this one who seemed to be a little "off the latch." But she didn't want to be left standing alone in the middle of nowhere, so she reluctantly climbed in behind Vera. The car rattled off down the road.

Vera blathered on and on to the driver, while Beth sat with mounting fear. The fellow in the front passenger seat was shaking his head and muttering to himself.

"Don't mind Curtis," yelled the driver above the engine's noise. "He's OK. He's a little shy around girls."

Suddenly, on hearing his name, Curtis turned around and leered at Beth with a huge drooling grin. His rubbery, wet lips slid back over an uneven row of tobacco-stained teeth. One arm flopped over the back of the seat, and his hand brushed against Beth's bare knee. He rubbed his dirty fingers over her skin. Horrified, Beth jerked her legs away. She pressed up against Vera, pulling her feet up onto the seat away from his groping hand. She remained curled up there until they reached the dirt road that led into Pine-Acres. As they approached the turn-off, Vera leaned over and shouted in the driver's ear. "Let us out here!" He stopped the car, and in one quick motion, reached around to lock the rear door. But Vera was too fast for him. She grabbed a wrench from the floor and slammed it down on his wrist. "Ow! Dammit!" he screamed. "You broke my wrist!"

He cradled his hand, groaning in pain. Curtis looked down at his brother's injured wrist that was already puffing up. He began to giggle, as if he held a secret joke. The girls fled from the car, stumbling down the dirt road. They didn't stop running until they reached Pine-Acres Resort.

Later, as they lay in their beds at Wilderness Lodge, Vera thought it all a huge joke. Her raucous laughter whipped the air like a sword.

"What a pair of freaks!" she screamed. "Did ya ever see anything so stupid when he locked the door? Lord! As if we'd have anything to do with THEM! And that other one that kept feeling your leg! He was a real sweetheart!" Vera fell back on her bed choking. Tears rolled down her cheeks. Beth was still trembling.

Hank and Johnny were a couple of years older than Vera and Beth. They teased the girls relentlessly, always hoping for a little encouragement in a romantic vein. The boys were also determined to have a good summer, and here were two willing greenhorns right under their noses.

One night, after they'd finished their chores, they borrowed a canoe from the slip where they were kept for the use of the guests. They invited Vera and Beth to a dance at Bide-a-Wee Lodge across the lake. As they paddled away from the dock at Wilderness Lodge, Beth noticed two blankets folded up in the bow and a bottle of Canadian Club half hidden between the folds. She poked Vera and looked at her with raised eyebrows. Vera just held up her hands and shrugged her shoulders in a "who knows?" gesture.

Hank tied up the canoe at the Bide-a-Wee dock while Johnny spread the blankets on a grassy patch near the dance hall. They passed around a "mickey" of rye half filled with ginger ale before Hank tucked it under a corner of the blanket. Vera was hopping around, impatient to get onto the dance floor. She boogied on ahead to the music booming out of the open door. Hank caught up to her and they waltzed inside, to join the frantic crowd on the dance floor. They bobbed and spun in a frenzied jitterbug, while the music of

Glenn Miller's "In the Mood" blared from the jukebox. As Hank swooped down, Vera flew over his shoulder, thrashing her legs in the air, her shrieks adding to the din. The crowd backed away and formed a circle around them, screaming and clapping to the rhythm and spurring them on with cries of "Go, go, go!" Gasping for breath Hank and Vera surged toward each other, and then retreated, never missing a beat. Between the music and the screaming crowd, the noise was deafening.

When the music stopped for an intermission, the exhausted pair dragged themselves outside. More than a little drunk, they flung themselves down on the blanket in the cool night breeze and drained what was left in the bottle that had been nearly emptied in their absence.

It was a different story for Johnny. The poor fellow was trying to help Beth, who had guzzled too much and was in an advanced state of drunkenness. He zigzagged onto the dock with his woozy partner clutching him for support. Suddenly Beth spewed it off the end of the dock like a gusher, and watched as it floated out into the lake like a multi-coloured pancake.

Well, that pretty much finished the night's revelry, and the four made a hasty retreat across the lake, the boys paddling furiously, and muttering in disgust. Beth's indiscretions had killed any romantic plans Johnny and Hank had hoped for. Usually after a good puke, a person feels better, but Beth just hung her head over the back of the canoe, leaving a wake of brown vomit floating behind. A drunken Vera stared at the gelatinous puddles.

"Look, Beth!" she shrieked, pointing to the bobbing mess. "You've left a trail!" Her peals of laughter rang out across the lake like a jackal in the night.

"You be Hansel and I'll be Gretel," she bellowed at Hank. "We'll follow the trail back!" But he just glared at her, and kept paddling. Beth lay draped over the side as they closed in on the welcome sight of Wilderness Lodge.

They half carried Beth to her room and dumped her on the bed.

"Am I home yet?" she mumbled, her voice as thick as molasses.

"Ohhhh," she groaned. "I feel awful." Then, mercifully, she was whirled into oblivion. Soon the rumbling sounds of snoring filled the room.

The next morning, Vera crossed the courtyard to the kitchen alone, looking crisp and fresh in her white apron and cap, despite the ravages of the night before. Beth was still buried under the covers.

It was up to Vera to concoct a believable lie for Mrs. Hunt, the Lodge's owner. Vera didn't want Beth to lose her job. Who knew what sort of boring person might replace her? Making the story up as she went along, she said that Beth had been feeling OK all evening, and then, in the middle of the night, she started throwing up. Vera was sure Beth had caught the flu.

"She likely got it from one of the guests," she assured Mrs. Hunt, who was already doubting the story. She knew all about Vera's escapades in the past. The young girl had worked at the Lodge for several summers, and her tall tales had aroused Mrs. Hunt's suspicions many times. But Vera was a good waitress, and good waitresses were hard to find, so Mrs. Hunt hired her back every year, hoping for some improvement in her behaviour.

Johnny and Hank busied themselves in the kitchen, and were quiet as they listened to the dialogue between Vera and Mrs. Hunt. They didn't want to be included in the story and risk losing their jobs.

When breakfast was over, and the few lingering guests had left the dining room, Vera hurried back to the staff annex. Beth was awake and propped up on her pillow. She looked like a warmed-up corpse. Gone was the bloom in her cheeks and the sparkle in her eyes of last night. She was suffering from a cracking hangover.

"How long have I been asleep?" Panic brought a little life to her eyes as she looked up at Vera.

"About 12 hours." Vera said smoothly. " Don't worry, Beth. I told Mrs. Hunt you've got the flu. The old dragon believed every word."

"Does she really believe it's the flu?" Beth whimpered.

"Well, I don't think she'd believe in the second coming," Vera scoffed, "but she won't fire us. It's too late in the season to find anyone else."

"Thank heavens," Beth groaned. She glanced up at Vera with a woeful look.

"When will I be better, Vera?" she pleaded.

"In about twenty-four hours. Guaranteed." Vera spoke like a pro. An amused smile hovered around her lips.

"I don't want to die," Beth's voice faded out.

"You ain't gonna die, kiddo." Vera looked down at her friend, prostrate with the stomach wambles. She smothered a grin and patted her head.

"Thanks, Vera," Beth mumbled and hunkered down in the bed under a lump of bedclothes. She drifted off to sleep again. Vera tiptoed from the room.

The next morning, Beth was back on the job in the dining room, serving breakfast to the guests under the watchful eye of Mrs. Hunt, who still wasn't convinced of Vera's story. As she went about her work, Beth silently mouthed the age-old mantra, I'll never get drunk again! I'll never get drunk again! I'll never get drunk again!

Years have passed since those episodes at the lodge, and now here we are, Beth and I, two women in our seventies, sitting on my verandah on a warm summer's afternoon, reminiscing and enjoying each other's company. We have remained as close as sisters can be, despite the great distances that have often separated us. I live in Tamarack, she in British Columbia She lives alone, widowed last year after forty-seven years of marriage. Today she is visiting me from her home in Victoria.

We talk, as we often do, of the time when we were young. We've been laughing and talking over old memories, just as our parents and relatives did so long ago on this same verandah. There are nearly seven years in age between us, so there are many things we never knew about each other. Today is the first time I've heard about her exploits at Wilderness Lodge. She's so mature and sensible, it's hard to believe she is the same person.

We fall into the private silence of remembering, looking at each other, but not seeing the two old women we've become, but only our laughing, youthful faces of yesterday.

"Remember this one, Mel?" she asks me. She's always called me Mel although my name is Melissa.

She begins to sing in a low, throaty voice as she rocked from side to side.

"Oh! playmate! Come out and play with me
And bring your dollies three
Climb up my apple tree
Shout down my rain barrel

Slide down my cellar door

And we'll be jolly friends

Forevermore!"

When she came to the part "Shout down my rain barrel," the urge to join in was irresistible and I sang along with her to the finish.

The Mourners

It was a rare day when Pat McClusky came to town. Pat was a prospector for a mining company up north. His home was a log cabin in the bush. He'd banged it together by himself for himself. He liked to live rough. He would never marry. There was no way he'd be a slave to any female barracuda. He'd come to town for the funeral of Harry Ferguson, his brother-in-law and good drinking buddy. Harry had recently succumbed to the ravages of time and whiskey. It was no surprise. Everyone knew he was overly fond of the "jug." Over his seventy-odd years, he'd been dried out more times than a hayfield in summer.

Pat stood on the corner shooting the breeze with his buddies. The funeral wasn't until 2:00 o'clock and he was having second thoughts about showing up for it.

"Howzit goin', Pat? Long time no see, eh buddy?" Mickey Byrne slapped Pat's shoulder. "I s'pose you come to the funer'l?"

"Ya, I tot I'd mosey inta town to pay me respecks to good old Harry."

"I seen him meself, just t'other day," Mickey went on. "In Finnegan's Hotel it was. That man had the death mask all right. I said to meself, 'Harry Ferguson's got the death mask!'"

"I s'pose he was potted, was he?" asked Tim O'Shea, blowing on his hands for warmth.

"Not at all," replied Mickey. "And that weren't the strangest part of it." Mickey looked from Tim to Pat. "He didn't say nothin' to me at all! I've known Harry Ferguson all me life and he didn't so much as give me a nod."

"Well, if he had the death mask that explains it, don't it?" Tim reasoned.

"Are ye no hearin' me, Tim? It t'were just the mask. He weren't a goner yet!"

"Well, he wouldn't be would he if you seen him in Finnegan's."

A puzzled frown formed on Mick's face. "Aw, Tim, would you not open yer ears! We ain't communicatin' here at all." He squinted down the road, his hand shading his eyes. "Hey Pat! Ain't that Maggie's car approachin'?"

Pat looked up and spotted his sister's new 1938 Chevy.

"Well, geez, if it ain't the Princess," he chuckled. "Hey, Maggie, hold up thar!" he roared. "I'm comin' with ya!" He lumbered toward the car. His red plaid mackinaw swung open. His rubber boots thumped against the pavement, leaving a trail of dried mud. He was hatless, his red hair ruffling in the breeze.

Maggie stopped the car when she saw her younger brother standing in the middle of the road flailing his arms about and shouting like a wild man. Pat pulled open the car door and stuck his head inside. The car was packed with their relations and they were all headed to the Temple Baptist Church for Harry's funeral.

"Well, now, it's all the grievin' kinfolk, is it!" Pat grinned a big toothy grin. "Waitin' for the will, are ya?" The sober looking group, wedged in like chickens in a cage, stared at him in astonishment. It had been a long time since they'd crossed paths, and it was never long enough for Pat.

His sister Maggie, (she called herself Margaret now), gave him a regimental inspection. "God Almighty, Pat!" she scolded. "Sure and you can't be goin' to Harry's wake looking like the divil hisself! Will you look at yourself now!"

"Oh, ho! Is it a woman's touch I'm needin', Maggie?" he teased, his blue eyes twinkling in his weathered face.

"It's more than a touch you're needin', boyo," she muttered. "More like a damn clout around the ears!"

"Sufferin' Jaysus, woman! Harry ain't gonna care about all that. He's already come to, what you might say, a definite conclusion! Them pallbearers ain't just rehearsin', you know!" He wagged his stubbled chin at her.

Maggie glared at him over the collar of her Persian lamb coat. The wide brim of her black hat shielded her scowling face.

"Get in," she muttered through clenched teeth. "And will you try to keep yourself out of sight, at all!"

"Hell! There ain't no room!" he roared.

"Ah, now, Paddy, auld son!" Cousin Jake spoke up from his seat beside Maggie. "Park yer arse in here beside yer sister. I'll squeeze inta the back between the ladies." His eyes held a mischievous gleam. The wary trio of women quickly pressed together to make room for him. Even though Jake was family, they'd agreed long ago that he was an ill-bred, vulgar galoot, and they made every effort to avoid him whenever possible.

Pat slid into the empty seat.

"Well now, Maggie darlin'", he said. "How are you old girl?"

He tried to give her a hug but she was in no mood for that. "Don't be butterin' me up either," she muttered shrugging him off. His unexpected appearance rattled her usual regal composure.

She stared at the rough sight of him. He might have tidied himself up a bit, she thought. Pat knew that look. That one of disapproval that she did so well. It popped up often when he was around her, that same steely glare that focused on Harry when he was alive and in a drunken stupor. Maggie pressed the accelerator and the car inched and shuddered down the street. She glanced at Pat out of the corner of her eye. She was thinking he hadn't changed much from the grubby little brother she remembered who liked to dig in the dirt.

A smile tugged at her lips. A sudden wave of fondness pushed aside her irritation for the moment. She thought back to the days when they were young and living at home on the farm and all the uproar he caused. Pat was an impulsive seventeen then. One afternoon he disappeared with the family Model T Ford. When he drove home the next morning, the whole top had been completely sheared off. His mother was so angry she decked him right there in the front yard with everybody watching. When he hit the ground all the kids cheered. The older boys began to chant, "Patty, Patty, dirty Mick!" The younger kids took up the chant shouting, "Dirty Mick! Dirty Mick!" Everyone thought he had it coming because he'd refused to take any of them on his wild spree. Nobody ever found out how he'd done it. He had more tales than the Arabian Nights, and they all fought each other for the truth.

In a moment of weakness Maggie made the suggestion that she knew he was waiting for. "I was wonderin' Pat, will you be comin' up to the house after for the funeral tea?" It was a half-hearted invitation, and she hoped he wouldn't show up.

"My God! There's a notion, Maggie! Sure! I'll be there! Wouldn't miss it! Will there be a bar, Maggie?" His grin widened. He knew what she was thinking. But there was no malice in Pat. He'd always had a soft spot in his heart for his older sister, who had been all but a mother to him.

Pat was the last of the McClusky brood, and his mother had already been driven nearly demented by her seven other little "darlins." Besides, Pat thought he owed it to Maggie and to Harry. When he and Harry got together at his cabin, and away from the watchful eye of Maggie, the two had enjoyed many a booze-up with what seemed like a never-ending supply of Jameson's, and beer chasers. Good old Harry was never one to stint on spirits.

"Pull up at the next corner, Princess. I wanta git meself a traveller." Pat pointed to the liquor store ahead. He knew it would be just like her to have a dry wake.

Maggie pursed her lips and kept driving.

"Hit the brakes, dammit, Maggie! Lemme out!"

Maggie jammed her foot on the brake pedal. The car screeched to a halt, flinging everyone forward. Pat pushed open the door and jumped out. He leaned inside, and in a soft voice said, "I'll sorely miss the old bugger!"

He slammed the door and sang out, "Abyssinia!"

Maggie sped away, the wheels spitting gravel.

~~

It was a cloudy and windy day in early March, the day of Harry's funeral. Those standing at the gravesite had been thoroughly chilled by the late winter cold, a penetrating dampness that seeped into their very bones. And now that the funeral was over, a dozen or so friends and relations gathered in Maggie's home warming themselves by the fire in the stone fireplace. They balanced cups of tea and little plates of sandwiches and cakes in their stiffened fingers.

Annie O'Hearne sat in corseted rigor in one of the straight-backed chairs brought from the dining room to accommodate the guests. She looked much older than her fifty-five years. She had a gaunt body and a long narrow face that was accentuated by her graying hair she'd pulled back in a tight bun at the nape of her neck. Her thin lips were pursed in a suitable mournful look. Maggie sat beside her, plump as a hen. Her full head of white hair had been freshly set the day before and she wore her best black suit.

Annie's eyes strayed to the window as she spoke to Maggie in a consoling tone. She could see the driveway easily. Her eyes widened.

"Jesus, Mary, and Joseph!" she whispered to Maggie. "It's Pat, comin' to the door!"

Maggie jerked upright, spilling her tea into the saucer.

"Is he sober then?" she asked.

"No, love, he's as tight as a tick and he's got that shiftless old Mickey Byrne with him. The pair of them can barely stand up on their pins!"

"God above!" Maggie made a move to get up. Her face was flushed with anger.

"Don't be stirrin' yourself, Margaret." Annie gently pressed her back into the chair. "I'll head them off!" She sprang to her feet and made it to the door just as Pat was reaching for the doorknob. She stepped outside and quickly closed the door against the prying eyes inside. She confronted the two revelers weaving on the stoop.

"Git yer sorry arses 'round to the back door, the pair of you," she snarled.

"Shtep a-shide, woman, we're goin' in!" Pat growled.

"Take one step, Pat McClusky, and you'll be kissin' dirt!" Annie kept her voice low but the threat was there all the same.

Pat glared at her out of bloodshot eyes. Pat was always a gentleman even when he was drunk. He would never hit a woman, at least that's what he told himself. Secretly he was afraid of women, but he would be the last person to admit it.

"C'mon, Mick. Do as the old battle-axe says." His voice slurred over the words. Arm in arm, they lurched toward the rear of the house and tottered up the steps.

Maggie met them at the kitchen door.

"Take your useless selves down to the cellar!" she said in a low voice. She opened the door and flicked on the light.

"If you'll bring us some whiskey and water, t'would be a comfort. I'm fair parched," Pat whined, wearing an expression of intense self-pity.

"I'll do nought!" Maggie scoffed. "It's tea you'll have and sure that's all you'll be gettin' here! You can come up when you're both sober and fit for human company."

"Jaysus, woman! You're bein' very depressin'," Pat muttered. Maggie shut the door and turned the key in the lock.

The pair sat grumbling in the cellar until the last of the visitors had left. When they'd sobered up enough to Maggie's satisfaction, she released them from their dank prison and ushered them to the back door where Annie was standing guard.

"Sure and it was a great pleasure to see you again, Pat," Maggie taunted. " The next time you come, will you try to arrange a state of sobriety?"

"Not a drop past me lips nor a crumb from yer hands," Pat muttered. "Yer a tyrant, Maggie Ferguson."

Maggie's shrill reprimands rang out as the two outcasts high-tailed it down the road at top speed.

Three, Four, Shut the Door

Since mid-morning Elly Scott sat motionless in the maroon velvet chair. The light in the room was dim. The lamps hadn't been turned on and night was closing in fast as it always did this time of the year in Tamarack. The house was still as if the very walls were listening, waiting for something to happen. She sat there, stiff, silent, bewildered as to what had become of her month-old infant. She thought she'd bathed Sophie. The little tub was still sitting on the kitchen table full of water, cold now with a bar of melting soap stuck to the bottom. And she thought she'd fed her. An empty bottle sat on the table beside her chair. But she couldn't remember what had happened after that. She tried to sort it all out, but reality kept drifting out of her reach. A small shape kept reappearing in her mind but she couldn't make it out. Each time it appeared, it was smaller than the time before, and now it had vanished altogether. She didn't know how many hours had passed since her husband, Ed, had left the house. She was there in body but her mind had crawled away and died.

When Ed had left for work that morning, Elly was clearing the breakfast table and stacking the dishes in the sink. She ran the hot water and threw in a handful of detergent to let them soak. Ed always left the house early and hardly ever got home before dusk, sometimes much later. He was the

Manager of The Bond Paper Mill in the town of Middleton, twenty miles distant. Sometimes Elly felt neglected by her husband, shut out of his life.

This morning she felt uneasy, a feeling she'd had most days since Sophie's birth. She was anxious about something she'd either forgotten to do, or was going to do. She wasn't sure which. Her anxiety had grown over the month since she'd come home from the hospital. This morning she couldn't seem to focus on anything. Nothing around her appeared as it was. It all floated away before she could grab onto it and reason it out. Sophie's crying was a screeching wail. It never stopped. It didn't matter what Elly did, the screaming went on and on and on until this morning she felt a cold rage spreading like a wave, growing until it reached every part of her body flowing through her veins like ice water.

"Stop it! Stop it!" Her voice rose. She dropped the plate into the sink and ran down the hall to the nursery. She grabbed up Sophie in her pink blanket, her tiny arms flailing in the air. "Stop it!" she screamed into the baby's red face. But Sophie didn't stop. She screamed louder, frightened by her mother's shouting. The cold fury surged through Elly. She was beyond rational thinking. All the sleepless nights, all the days with never a moment to rest, and the baby's screaming this morning, had tipped her over the edge and driven her to sitting in the twilight alone and empty of all recollection.

"I'm home, Elly!" Ed called as he poked his head into the living room. He thought she was asleep. Sometimes he'd find her like that in the chair. The house was quiet. He tiptoed down the hall to the little nursery as he always did when he came home. He'd gather up "Sweetie," his pet name for his little girl, and carry her into the living room where he and Elly would play with her, marvelling over her tiny hands and fingers, so small, so perfect.

But Sophie wasn't in her crib. A growing awareness that something was not right sent Ed rushing back to Elly.

He stared down at her, his eyes full of fear. His voice was low and deliberate. "Elly! Where is Sophie?" Elly didn't look at him.

"Elly! Elly! Where is Sophie?" His voice grew louder and he shook her shoulder.

Elly looked up. Her pale face was tight, her eyes vacant. Ed knelt down beside her rubbing her cold hands in his.

"Look at me, Elly," he whispered. "What's happened to you?" He stroked her arms trying to coax some response from her.

A door in Elly's mind cracked open. A flash of insight brought a low groan from her tightly pressed lips. She stared at Ed. Her eyes were wild. Her face was ashen.

"The stove!" she mumbled her voice barely audible. She closed her eyes and began to moan in anguished inhuman sounds as she rocked back and forth in the chair.

"The stove? What about the stove?" Ed gasped. The blood drained from his face. His voice was hoarse. His fear was suffocating him.

"My God! Elly! What have you done?" But Elly had slipped silently through a little door that clicked shut behind her and where Ed could not follow.

The fire in the kitchen stove was dying out. Ed was shaking as he bent down to open the firebox. Beads of panic gathered on his forehead. He brushed the tears from his eyes. The sight before him drove him to his knees, his head in his hands. Hoarse sounds rumbled from his throat. With trembling fingers he tugged on a corner of the pink blanket, scorched and smoldering. A tiny blackened hand slid out of the folds, fingers fanned out in a cry for help. The gruesome scene punched Ed in the pit of his stomach like a fist and he retched. In seconds his face became that of an old man. For long minutes he sat motionless on the cold floor. He tried to capture his racing thoughts. He knew what he had to do. He had to take his little girl out from her smoldering grave. He reached in and gently pulled the blanket toward him. Ashes floated softly to the floor. Bits of charred pink cloth clung to his fingers. He pulled out the tiny bundle and held it against his shoulder. It felt warm against his cold body. Soot from the blanket smudged his shirt collar. He could feel the small lifeless shape as he held it close to his heart. It smelled of singed hair and burnt flesh.

He stumbled into the living room where Elly sat her eyes wide and empty. Ed held out the scorched bundle to her, but she didn't see it. She was deep in her lonely, silent world. He laid Sophie's small body on the sofa and moved like a man underwater to the telephone.

"This is Ed Scott," he said to Mavis Cooke, the receptionist. "I have to speak to Dr. Mills at once!" His hands were shaking so much he could barely hang onto the receiver. Mavis's voice came over the line.

"I'll have him call you Ed, he's with a patient right now. What's the trouble?" she asked. Ed hung up. His whole body was numb as he stared at Elly. Then the ringing telephone dispelled his stupor.

"Doctor! Our baby – burned – in the stove! Elly, she's not moving! Oh, God! Little Sophie! All burned!"

"Ed, I'm driving right over. I don't want you to do anything. Just wait for me." Within minutes Dr. Mills was coming through the door.

"My God, Ed! What's happened? Sit down. Tell me everything."

Ed tried to collect his thoughts.

"I don't know any more than I told you on the phone. I can't get a word out of Elly. She's lost, Doctor.

Completely lost. I don't know what to do! Our baby, our little Sophie! She's gone!" His voice broke into sobs.

Dr. Mills put a consoling arm around Ed's shoulders.

"Take it easy, Ed. I'll have a look at Sophie first." He went into the living room where Elly was sitting bolt upright, her eyes squeezed shut. The baby was on the sofa. Dr. Mills carefully unwrapped the little bundle and his stomach churned at the sight. His eyes filled with tears as he looked down at the baby's dark, blistered skin. He'd never seen anything like this in all his years of practice. He gave the tiny body a brief examination. An autopsy would determine if the fire had been the exact cause of death. He turned to Elly who had slipped behind a black curtain and into another world. He checked her pulse and heart. He lifted her eyelids and shone a small light into her eyes that were darting back and forth in frantic motion.

"Call an ambulance, Ed. She's in shock. We've got to get her into the hospital immediately."

Ed ran to the phone. He shouted his name and address to the dispatcher.

"Get me an ambulance right away. It's an emergency!"

He slammed down the receiver and staggered toward Dr. Mills who was standing in the doorway slowly shaking his head. The whole scene was inconceivable. He tried to concentrate on Ed weaving before him dazed.

"Now, Ed," he said as he tried to get him to focus. "We must call the police."

"No, no, not the police!" Ed protested.

"We have to report this, Ed, because of the circumstances. It's the law, you see." He saw Ed's despair.

"My dear fellow. Elly won't be arrested or anything like that. Don't worry. I'll make the call."

Ed slumped into a chair, his head bowed. The doctor put his hand on Ed's shoulder.

"I'll speak to Chief Atkinson myself," he said quietly. "Here's the ambulance now, Ed. Go with Elly and I'll follow you in my car after I've talked to the Chief."

Two attendants carried Elly on a stretcher to the waiting ambulance. Ed turned to look at the little bundle lying on the sofa.

"Go on, Ed. I'll see that everything is taken care of here. Stay with Elly. I'll meet you later at the hospital." Ed walked stiffly to the waiting ambulance and climbed in. Elly lay inside on the stretcher, rigid as death.

As the ambulance pulled away, Dr. Mills picked up the phone and dialed the police station. He asked for Chief Atkinson.

"George, it's Dan Mills here. I'm at Ed Scott's house. I have a tragic case on my hands here. Their baby is dead."

"Good Lord! What happened?"

"I really don't know. Ed came home from work and discovered the baby in the woodstove. Burned. Ghastly business, George. Looks like infanticide. Elly is in shock and on her way to the hospital with Ed."

"I'll be right there, Dan!"

Moments later Chief Atkinson came in. Two policemen followed him. They examined the baby and after a quick look through the house left for the hospital to talk to Ed. Dr. Mills wrapped the body tenderly in a sheet and carried it out to his car.

~~

The circumstances of Sophie's death were hushed up as much as you could ever keep anything quiet in Tamarack. Folks whispered about it and it wasn't long before the whole ugly incident was out in the open. People felt sorry for Ed, and for Elly too, saying that if she'd been in her right mind, she'd never have done such a horrible thing. But Mrs. Graham, who always seemed to have her nose into everybody's business, wouldn't let it go. She prattled on about her opinions to anyone who would listen. "I always thought the girl was a little odd and I'm not at all surprised," she declared. "That time I brought a chicken casserole over when she had that little sweetheart Sophie. I thought she would appreciate it. Just grabbed it out of my hands and muttered something. I don't know what. And then she shut the door in my face! Can you imagine that! Never did get my dish back neither!"

Sophie's funeral was attended by nearly everyone in Tamarack. Most were there to offer their support to the young couple, but some came out of curiosity, just to see what a real murderer looked like. But if that was their intent, they were disappointed. Elly was unable to attend her daughter's funeral. She remained hospitalized and untouched.

The autopsy and the police investigation proved that Elly, in a deep psychotic state, had thrust her child into the stove where she'd burned to death. A Provincial Court Judge declared Elly mentally unfit to stand trial. Attempts by psychiatrists to assess her mental state were thwarted by her continuing psychosis. She lay in her hospital bed unaware of the dreadful part she had played in her baby's death.

At Sophie's funeral, Ed stood beside the tiny white casket. Neighbours crept silently up to him. They said things he barely heard, but somehow he was able to murmur the proper responses. When it was all over, Dr. Mills drove Ed home.

"Do you want some company for a little bit, Ed?" he asked.

"No, I don't think so, doctor. I appreciate everything you've done, but I just want to be alone now if you don't mind."

"Of course, Ed. I understand. Just call if you feel a need to talk. And Ed," he added, "remember the whole town is with you. Don't shut us out."

Ed shook the doctor's hand and stepped out of the car. He hesitated at his front door before going inside. He felt exhausted and as empty as the house. But something kept nagging him. Was he partly to blame for Elly's descent into madness? Could she have known? He unlocked the door and walked slowly into the kitchen. He stumbled down the hall to Sophie's bedroom, bent over the crib and picked up her teddy bear. He pressed it to his face as though he could bring it to life. Then he threw it into the crib, crept into the living room and sank into the maroon chair. A hair - a fine gold hair - Elly's. He picked it up and began to weave it through his fingers over and over, hour by hour until darkness shrouded the room. And when he could no longer stand the silence he raised his arm, reached for the phone and dialed a number. A woman's voice answered. Ed cleared his throat. "Louise? Honey?"

The Perfect Lady

"Albert is dead!" The words rang in my head like the Liberty Bell. All I could think of was Aggie, my cousin. Now she was free of him. Her years of humiliation and betrayal were finally over. The anger I'd felt toward Albert Hendrickx was over too, and now I could bury him and all the unwanted advances that he'd forced on me when I was a young girl.

Although it has been many years since Albert tried to seduce me, I will never forget how he used to sneak up on me as I was making tea in Aggie's kitchen when she had taken to her bed with one of her migraines. He would grab me from behind and cup his filthy hands around my breasts pressing me back against the hardness of his body.

"Let go of me, Albert," I would threaten. "I'll tell my father on you!" He would just back away with that arrogant smile.

"Don't worry, I'll get you yet," he'd whisper.

One day when I was about fifteen years old he stopped bothering me. I can only think that maybe Aggie got wind of what he was up to and, for once in her life, she'd laid down the law. If she knew about his tom-catting around with other women, that was one thing, but molesting her young cousin was something she would never tolerate.

Today, many years later, his body lies stiff and cold in a fancy casket in the parlour of the family home. He's all dressed up in a navy blue suit, a red tie knotted around his scrawny neck. I feel nothing as I look down at his shrunken body, his cold bloodless hands clasped together across his chest.

"Well, Albert," I whisper, "you don't look like much now."

By some miracle he'd survived forty years of debauchery. My father always said that Albert would "hiccup his way to heaven."

The cloying smell of floral sprays with their overpowering sweetness sickens me. I want to look at the little cards tucked into the petals, to see who could possibly feel enough compassion for Albert to remember him with flowers. But I turn away and move toward Aggie, whose tiny frame is swallowed up in a huge, gold damask wing chair. Her real name is Agnes Rose. Her mother never called her anything else, but the family has called her Aggie since she was a little girl.

Today her two daughters, Cora and Amy, flank their mother like the Imperial Guard. Neither of them ever married. They both have that intense, anxious look that some women get when they long for a man and marriage and worry that they're too old to attract one. Any hope they'd had faded away long ago. They're both well past middle age. They stayed on in the family home, caring for their mother. Albert had always said the girls were Aggie's business, and he took very little part in their upbringing. The sisters seemed content with their lives, even though they'd both been left "hanging on the vine," so to speak.

Some said that Aggie had been selfish keeping them from a life with a husband and children. But I say there are worse things in life than not being married. Maybe they'd never been asked. If there's any beauty there at all, it's well hidden. They don't favour their mother's fair and delicate features. Both girls are sallow-skinned, with thick dark brows and straight black hair. They take after their father in looks, more's the pity. Nor has nature been kind by endowing them with thick waists, heavy bosoms, and limbs that would make a Steinway proud. But both have been blessed with Aggie's sweet temperament. Intelligent and well read, they're an interesting pair to engage in conversations on almost anything worth talking about.

When Albert died two days ago, it was said that he'd died of a heart attack brought on by "excitement." That soon became the town joke. Everyone knew he'd been found in his cabin, after a frantic phone call to the police from a woman who refused to give her name. She would only tell where they could find him, and quickly hung up when the constable pressed her for details. It seemed that Albert had died the way he wanted to.

I join the long line of callers whispering their condolences and moving somberly past Aggie as though they really cared about old Albert. I watch my proper cousin as she shyly greets the mourners. I can see the questioning tilt of her head that has always served to shift the attention from herself as though you might find out something about her that she didn't want you to know. Her mouth is as frozen as a cherry popsicle. Neither her lips nor her eyes give anything away. She looks the perfect lady, smiling and nodding to everyone even though she can't hear what is said. Deaf as a stone she is. She hasn't heard a clap of thunder in years.

Incredible as it seems, Aggie has remained untouched by all the public scandals that lingered around Albert like a whiff of manure. None were ever proven, but the gossip persisted in the village. A few times, Albert found himself jailed overnight for being drunk and disorderly in the Lido Hotel. But nothing ever came of that, except maybe to cause a stir in the family graveyard.

Folks called him "Greasy," because he was always able to slip out of any scrapes he got into. Nothing seemed to stick to him. Albert's acceptance in the town lay in the pity everyone felt for his wife.

The truth was that Albert and some of his unscrupulous friends had a thriving bootlegging business that they operated out of Albert's cabin on Trout Lake, a few miles from town. Some even said they had a "kept" woman working there. "Theresa-something" it was rumoured. A well-endowed young woman. Nobody knew her last name.

When anyone spoke of her they rudely called her "Miss Bountiful-up-the-street-there." She lived with her grandfather, in an old house on the main street. Some suspected that Theresa had a prosperous business of her own going on in Albert's cabin, an arrangement she'd had with him in exchange for running the business. But that was never proven for sure either. Certainly, her customers would never tell.

While gossip swirled around Albert, Aggie shielded herself in a kind of fantasy world. She rose above all the tittle-tattle, buried all the gossip and bolted the door shut. She kept her dignity in spite of all the humiliations Albert continued to heap upon her. Folks thought she should have thrown him out years ago, but we all knew that the only way she would part with Albert would be feet first out of the parlour and in a box!

Did Aggie know the truth about Albert and his ties to young Theresa? If she did, she never let on. She always treated him with respect, as if he were a proper gentleman instead of the old fool that he was. It sickened me whenever I heard her calling him "lover." That miserable old goat, and her calling him "lover!"

Over the years, Aggie's devotion to Albert was unwavering. She bought him the finest suits available, and just about anything else he wanted in the local "Dads and Lads" haberdashery. But as far as I was concerned, the old adage still rang true - "you can't make a silk purse out of a sow's ear."

It was a mystery how those two ever got together. It was about fifty years ago that Albert first arrived on Aggie's doorstep. He was a young man then in his early twenties. The story was that he'd been a deck-hand on a Belgian freighter, and that he'd jumped ship in Montreal and made his way north ending up in Tamarack. If the story were true, it would explain his unusual name, and his faint accent. Nobody in the town was really sure who he was, or where he came from. But that made him all the more appealing to the young and innocent Aggie. All she knew was that she wanted him. He courted her right off, over her father's objections, and shortly after they married. It was hinted that he hadn't married her for love, but because of love's consequences, and the battle royal he'd had with Aggie's outraged father.

And then there was that silver-framed picture that stood on his bureau. It was an old-fashioned photograph of a pretty dark-haired child with large soulful eyes. Once when Aggie showed it to me, she said it was a picture of Albert's niece. But the resemblance to him was so strong, it made me suspicious. She looked enough like Cora and Amy to be their sister. But the mystery stayed locked up in his bedroom. If Aggie knew the secret, she never told anyone.

With a start, I come back to myself in front of Aggie. I take her small hand in mine and bend to kiss her soft cheek.

I can smell her perfume. Lavender. A delicate, floating scent that suits Aggie's old-fashioned bearing.

"What a sad day for you, Aggie." I murmur the usual funereal comforts. I notice with envy that there's hardly a wrinkle on her pretty face. Her hair has turned from blonde to silver, and has been freshly arranged in deep waves like a ploughed field, and lacquered to a stiffness that would've held in a cyclone. She's all fussed up in a mauve silk dress, trimmed with an ecru lace collar and cuffs. A long strand of pearls hangs to her waist. Her fingers glitter with the diamond and sapphire rings left to her by her long-deceased mother. Albert had always bragged that he'd bought the rings as tokens of his love for Aggie. But I'd always known where they came from. I'd seen them on her mother's hands many times.

Aggie raises her head. "Thank you for coming," she says in a whispery voice. Her red lips part in a faint smile, and I notice that her crimson lipstick is beginning to creep into the fine lines above her lip. She's been repeating the same words over and over like a mantra, and I don't think she really sees me.

I drift into the background and sit down in one of the over-stuffed chairs and listen to the quiet chatter of the milling crowd. The room always looks to me like a New Orleans bordello, or how I imagine one would look. Heavy gold velour drapes hang at the long windows. Tiffany lamps sit on spindly carved tables, and red velvet Victorian loveseats fill up the space. A magnificent white marble clock, decorated with golden cherubs graces the mantel. The sweeping brass pendulum grimly marks time, as it chimes away the hours. The unlit fireplace is decorated in delft tiles in scenes of blue windmills and delicate Dutch landscapes. A huge flower arrangement sits on the hearth. Paintings fight for space on the walls. Many years ago Aggie's mother had owned the stylish furnishings. Now it all belonged to Aggie, including all the money her father had left her. In the midst of it all, she sits serenely, surrounded by her belongings, a repository of memories, some good, some bad, the remnants of her life.

As I watch the parade of mourners, my thoughts drift back many years to that awful day I spent with Albert. I was about seventeen then. Albert had just turned thirty. He had to go to Middleton. The mayor of the town had called Albert for a case of whiskey for an upcoming soiree in the council chambers. Tamarack was a "dry town", and the residents had to get their spirits elsewhere.

Albert had wanted to take along one his daughters to give his trip an air of respectability. But Cora and Amy had other plans for the day, arrangements they'd no doubt made in a hurry since neither had any desire to be part of their father's shady business dealings. The girls knew all about his reputation, but they never talked about him to anyone, not even to their mother. In those days one's family improprieties were kept hush-hush, and people lived their lives pretending they didn't exist.

When Albert couldn't find anyone to accompany him on his trip, he approached me. I wanted to go to Middleton very badly. There was a movie playing there that I desperately wanted to see. It was "Gone with the Wind" with my favourite actor, Clark Gable and this was the only chance I'd get to see it for weeks. And since Albert hadn't tried any funny business with me for over two years, I thought he'd behave himself. The thought of seeing that movie was uppermost in my mind.

After much coaxing on my part, my parents reluctantly agreed to let me go with him. I'd never told them about all the earlier scuffles I'd had with him, or they would never have allowed it. Make no mistake, there was heavy discussion between my mother and father about the trip. In those days, families were strongly connected, and loyalty was absolute. My parents were very fond of Aggie, and would never want to offend her by refusing to have anything to do with her "beloved" Albert. In the end, their affection for her overcame their misgivings, and the trip was arranged.

On a bright, sunny morning in early September, Albert and I set out for Middleton. He drove his new, 1932 maroon Buick. I can still recall its new-car smell and the softness of the gray plush seats. Albert had chosen the car, and Aggie's money had paid for it. But since she'd never learned to drive, Albert always regarded it as his.

As we sped along the highway, I scarcely noticed the passing countryside. I'd always made a point of not getting too close to him. Now I felt a little uncomfortable sitting beside him. He kept his eyes on the road. I sat in silence.

"Glad you commin' wit' me, Melissa. I always like you da best," he said in his faint accent. He gave me a sidelong glance as he reached over and patted my hand. I felt my heart pound as I met his eyes. I jerked my hand away. He was grinning. It was that same sinister, arrogant look he'd always had about him. All the gossip I'd ever heard about him started to take over my thoughts. I'd never asked my parents anything about him. In those days children didn't ask embarrassing questions about family members.

Over the miles, I didn't have much to say to him, and I wished we'd hurry up and get to Middleton. He'd given up any attempt at conversation with me, and lapsed into a tuneless whistling between his teeth. I pretended to be asleep.

After an hour or so of silence, Albert turned off the main highway and pulled into the town of Middleton. He drove into the parking lot behind the Albion Hotel. He turned to me and lightly touched my arm. I shrank back against the seat.

"I be about two hours, honey," he said as he looked at his watch. It was the expensive one Aggie had given him for his birthday two weeks before.

"Meet me here at de Albion." He pointed to the hotel. "Say, two-tirty, OK?"

"Oh!" I exclaimed. "Two-thirty won't be enough time! I was going to go to the movies!"

"I won't be here long enough for dat, Melissa. I'll be at the Albion, two-tirty, ready to go home. So you'd better be der." He gave a warning scowl.

I scrambled out of the car, resisting the impulse to run down the street. I had the eerie feeling he was standing by the car watching me. I rounded the corner onto Queen Street and slowed down to a stroll, pausing to look in the store windows. I was disappointed but more relaxed now that I was away from him. I couldn't halt the feeling that I had made a big mistake, now that my plan had fizzled out.

In Walker's Dry Goods store, I spent a long time looking for little gifts, finally choosing two lace handkerchiefs, one for my mother and one for Aggie. I paid the clerk and left to window-shop along the street. I hadn't much money left, so I decided to wait in Aikens Drug Store until two-thirty. I selected the latest Movie Mirror from the magazine stand, perched on a stool at the lunch counter and ordered a chocolate soda. I flipped through the pages and started to read. I forgot all about Albert as I buried myself in the lives of movie stars. The time slipped by, and with a start, I realized I had better get back to the Albion. If Albert got drinking he might forget I was with him, and drive off without me. I hurried along the street to the hotel.

When I opened the door I saw him sitting at a table by himself, flirting with the waitresses. As soon as I looked at him, I knew he had been drinking. His face was flushed, and his eyes were bloodshot. His red nose was swollen and stood out like a beacon. The thought of driving home with him in his drunken condition filled me with dread. I pretended to be friendly, despite my anxiety.

"Hi! I hope I'm not late, Albert." He shook his head and mumbled something in a slurred voice. My alarm edged up a notch.

"How about some coffee before we start for home?" I said, forcing a smile. He nodded and signaled to a waitress. I prayed the coffee would be strong enough to offset the whiskey.

As I looked across the table at him, I could see Albert wasn't an unhandsome man. He'd kept himself in pretty good shape, in spite of his high living. He'd always had the pick of the girls in town. There was something charismatic about him, some hidden secret about himself that seemed to draw women to him like flies to a rotten apple. His black hair shone in the light, and his dark, searching eyes seemed to look right through me, stripping the clothes from my body.

Little needles of fear shot through me. Suddenly he smiled, his teeth gleaming a brilliant white in his swarthy face. I looked away not wanting him to catch me staring and think I was flirting with him. His voice was thick and faltering.

"By de way, Melissa, I'm goin' to stop at de cabin. I get you home before dark, don' worry," he added, seeing my anxious look. I knew I had no choice. But I felt my stomach churn. Why did he want to stop there? It was getting late and close to dinnertime and I just wanted to get this trip over with and go home. I wouldn't go near his cabin no matter what he said!

As we drove along the highway, I forced myself to talk to him. He was going on about Aggie, and what a wonderful person she was, and how much he loved her. All I could think of was what a liar he was.

We turned onto a dirt road bordering Trout Lake and drove on to his small log cabin. Albert had built the cabin in the woods a few years ago. He seemed to spend more time there with his friends than he did at home with his family.

It was a desolate part of the country. Heavy trees lined the gravel road with just barely enough room to pass another car. We didn't see anyone along the way. My uneasiness grew. Albert pulled into a small clearing near the cabin.

"C'mon in, Melissa," he said. "We look inside. OK? See if any raccoons was stoppin' by. Rotten little buggers make big mess." He opened the car door and hesitated for a moment.

I started to tell him that I'd wait in the car, when the cabin door flew open, and a young girl stood framed in the shadows. It was Theresa! When she caught sight of Albert, her broad face beamed. But when she saw me sitting in the car her smile faded into a dark scowl. She stood rooted in the doorway. Her long black hair streamed down her back and over her bare shoulders, as straight as a waterfall. The fading sun caught the luminous, green shadow on her eyelids. She was short and plump, and very young. About my age, I guessed. She wore a pair of jeans as tight as a second skin, and a pink halter that barely covered her ample bosom. Her bare feet were firmly planted on the threshold. She was so surprised she was unable to move.

My mouth fell open. I'd always suspected that there was some truth to the gossip I'd heard about the two of them. Now I was sure of it. All I could think of was Aggie, waiting anxiously for the bum to come home.

"Albert," Theresa shouted from the doorway, "I didn't know you was comin' today!" She glanced suspiciously from Albert to me and back. He looked like a trapped rat. His black eyes darted frantically for an escape. He turned to me, apparently feeling a need to explain, but he only succeeded in looking foolish.

"Sometime Theresa comes to clean da cabin. I don' tink she's here today." He stared down at his feet as if he was afraid to face me. "She don' livin' here, if you tinkin' dat, Melissa," he added. He looked up, his eyes almost pleading.

Then, abruptly, he turned aside and leaped out of the car like a frightened deer. He half ran toward the cabin door, where Theresa was standing motionless. I couldn't see his face, but I could tell by his swift stride that he was very angry.

"Wha' da 'ell you doin' here?" he roared at her. "I don' wan you comin' here 'less I tell you!" His shouts echoed in the quiet woods. His fists were clenched in fury. He'd been caught red-handed. He knew I didn't like him much and probably thought I would rush to tell Aggie the moment I got home.

Theresa gawked at him for a long moment, speechless. Then she tossed her head and shouted, "You can't come in you lousy bastard! I'm busy!" And in one quick movement, she turned her back on him, stepped into the cabin, and slammed the door in his face.

It was sweet revenge to see him standing there, eyes red and bulging, completely dumbfounded. By this time, most of my fear had melted away and I covered my mouth to keep from laughing. Albert was finally knocked off his perch. And by a little slip of a girl almost young enough to be his daughter!

He climbed into the car and slammed the door. He was breathing heavily, sucking air between his teeth. I watched him out of the corner of my eye, biting my lips to keep from smiling. He didn't say a word as he tramped on the accelerator, and the car sped forward spitting dust and pebbles behind us. It was in my mind to ask, 'What about the raccoons, Albert?' but he was so angry I thought it wiser to hold my tongue.

He drove for a long time, whistling softly through his teeth and frowning at the road ahead. I kept an uneasy silence and stared out of the window. I could see his reflection in the glass. His face was dark and sullen. After a few miles, he turned to me and growled, "Ven ve get home and you see Aggie, I don' wan' you tellin' her nuttin' about Theresa. D'ya hear me, Melissa?" He glared over at me.

It was a threat, no denying it, and it put the fear of the devil in me.

"OK, Albert," I answered quickly. "I won't say a word to anyone."

I kept my word and, to this day, I've never told anyone about it. Whatever Albert had in his scheming mind for me that day, was squelched when Theresa appeared on the scene. And although she never knew it, I've always felt grateful to her.

~~

Now the voices in the parlour swell louder and I see Aggie's gleaming head coming towards me. She perches like a little silver bird beside me on the red velvet sofa and taking my hand in hers, she murmurs, "It's good to see you, Melissa. I'm glad you came. But then, I knew you would. You were always my favourite." She gives my hand a little squeeze.

"You know, dear," she went on, "I still have that pretty lace handkerchief you gave me so long ago. Do you mind the day when my poor dear Albert took you to Middleton? I've always kept your thoughtful little gift for special occasions. See? I have it tucked in my sleeve right now." Gently she draws it out and holds it up. "It's a lovely keepsake, and it reminds me of what a dear person you are." Her lips brush my cheek and she smiles a sweet, conspiring little smile. "Thank you, Melissa, for being so considerate," she whispers.

It was then I guessed she'd always known my secret about Albert and Theresa. Did the old fool finally tell her about all the skeletons in his closet before he exited this world? Aggie will never tell.

Dave's Brave New World

She'd prayed and prayed that it would all end soon. But the days crept by with the speed of a snail. Then on May 8, 1945, V.E. Day, the butchery stopped. A telegram arrived from Dave – "Home September 2nd, 1400 hours. Love you." Signed, Dave Bellemore." At two o'clock today Thelma's husband would be at Tamarack station.

"Oh, my God! He's finally coming home! How can I wait until two o'clock! Oh, I want so desperately to see him and to hold him in my arms!" She read the long awaited words over and over, pressing the telegram to her breast.

She danced and twirled around the tiny apartment in her nightgown, waving the paper in the air and shouting "Thank you, thank you!" to the empty rooms that had been so unbearably silent since Dave had gone away. Soon the small apartment would be filled with Dave's noisy fun-loving presence and his boyish vitality.

It had been nearly four years since their wedding, and they were together for only a month before he'd shipped out with his regiment to England. They'd known each other since high school and had been dating since their final year. It was no surprise to their friends when they married before Dave went off to the war.

Thelma moved around the apartment restlessly, puttering at this and that, picking up little trinkets and immediately replacing them. She lifted Dave's photo from the piano, gave it a kiss, and dusted his smile with her fingertips.

Will he have changed? she wondered. Dear God! I hope after all these years apart he still loves me.

Like Scarlett, in "Gone With the Wind," Thelma decided she would deal with all that later, when and if the time came. There was much to do before she could meet his train. She spent a long time bathing and daydreaming. She'd bought a special soap for a special occasion, "Yardley's Roses, Roses." She washed her long auburn hair, towelling it until it gleamed like new copper pennies and setting it in brown rollers. She cold-creamed her smooth face, and carefully coloured her nails with a crimson polish. When she had finished, she curled up in a chair with a steaming cup of tea, and fantasized about a happy life ahead with her beloved Dave.

Suddenly, the front door slammed. She heard a thump on the hall floor. Thelma spun around. Dave's khaki-clad figure filled the archway. Without a word, he held out his arms. Curlers and cold-cream were forgotten as Thelma flew into his embrace. He lifted her up and whirled her around and around, holding her tightly to him.

"Stop! Stop!" she cried, laughing and crying at the same time. "I'm getting dizzy!" He lowered her gently to the floor and stood looking into her face remembering every little freckle and dimple. Then he kissed her long and gently, his lips holding her to him. Dave tried hard to hold his emotions in check, but the exquisite joy of finally being home with his wife was too much. Suddenly the tears rolled down his weathered cheeks, now fragrantly smeared with cold cream. Sticky splotches had rubbed off on his uniform jacket, but Dave didn't care about any of that. He was home, with his wife in his arms, and that was all that mattered.

"Darling, darling Thel. I've missed you so much! I thought of you every day. Oh God! I love you so much!" he murmured hoarsely. Words that Thelma had waited so long to hear. They wept openly with happiness and relief, their tears mingling as they pressed close together.

"You were supposed to come at two o'clock," Thelma blubbered into Dave's chest. "Look at me! I'm a sight!" Her hands flew up to cover her burning cheeks, as she remembered the face cream, the ugly curlers.

Dave grinned down at her. "You're a sight all right, Thel. A sight for sore eyes! It's so good to be home, sweetheart. There were times when I wondered if I would ever see you again…" His voice drifted off. He tossed his cap onto a nearby chair, and rested his wet face against Thelma's slippery cheek. He pulled her so close she could hardly breathe. After a few minutes, he held her away a little and laughing, said, "Honey! Why are we both crying? I'm home now for keeps!" He scooped her up in his arms and they danced around the room shouting and laughing until they collapsed on the sofa, gasping for breath.

The next few days were idled away in a glow of rediscovering each other. The hours were sprinkled with the tears and laughter of two lovers who had been separated for too long. Dave caught up on all the news. Thelma now knew that Dave hadn't stopped loving her. They talked and talked and in a trembling voice, Dave said, "Thel, there were times in the last four years that I can't tell you about, at least not yet." She didn't want to ask him any questions about the war. She was determined not to make him relive it all over again and spoil the sweetness of his homecoming.

"Don't worry about all that, sweetheart," she said. "I'm just glad you're here with me now." She would wait until he was ready to tell her what he wanted her to know.

The days drifted by in a golden haze of passion and the companionship of just being together again.

Dave knew right off that he had to find work, and he joined the hundreds of other veterans in the country struggling to find a place in the workforce. He and Thelma scoured the newspaper ads every day.

Dave could have gone to college under the rehabilitation plan for veterans, but he wanted to get a job and have a regular paycheck. He was anxious to return to civilian life, to have a home and raise a family with Thelma. What's more, he wasn't sure he could settle down to books and the routine of study after all the turmoil of the last four years.

One morning, as they sat at the breakfast table, Dave saw a classified ad in the daily paper from the Heart O'Gold Collection Agency. They were looking for an able-bodied man to do their legwork collecting from customers who hadn't kept up their payments. Dave figured he was as able-bodied as the next guy, and had the wit for a job that seemed to be pretty cut and dried. So he set up an interview for the following morning.

Thelma pressed his white shirt, and his only suit that had hung in the closet for four years waiting for Dave's return. It was the blue serge he'd worn at his wedding. In the four years of army life, Dave had developed a tough, muscular physique, and the suit had become as tight as sausage skins. His shirt collar was like a noose around his neck. He unbuttoned it under his red and blue striped tie for fear if left fastened he would sound like a croaking frog.

"Well," he mused, "it will just have to do. There's no money right now for new clothes." Saul Ginsberg at the Dads and Lads Haberdashery wouldn't extend credit with just a hope that Dave would find work. "Business is business," was Saul's motto.

At ten o'clock the next morning, Dave was at the Heart O'Gold Agency for the interview. After a brief discussion, the Manager, Mr. Flint, hired him on the spot at seventy-five dollars a week. Dave was elated. A good job! And a good salary to start! He could hardly wait to tell Thelma.

At home, Thelma waited impatiently for Dave's return. Out of nowhere, a childish chant flashed through her mind. She repeated it aloud.

"Star light, star bright

First star I've seen tonight"

The front door flew open.

"I got it, Thel! I got the job!" Dave shouted.

"I knew you would," Thelma yelled, rushing out to meet him. "Who could resist such a handsome devil." She flew at him, throwing herself into his arms, and smothering him with kisses.

The afternoon drifted by as they basked in their good fortune. To celebrate, they'd have a nice dinner at the Mount Vesuvius Restaurant. It had been their favourite haunt before the war. The Mount Vesuvius was an Italian neighbourhood eatery where most of the patrons knew each other and met regularly. Welcoming shouts greeted Dave and Thelma as they came in the door. Luigi, the owner, came running toward them embracing them with rib-cracking hugs. He brought a bottle of Chablis to their table to celebrate Dave's safe return and all the patrons stood up and toasted the happy couple.

They ordered dinner and talked about Dave's future at his new job with the collection agency. He was wearing his snugly fitting blue suit, and Thelma was all dressed up in a blue flowered dress trimmed with a black, lacy peplum. She wore the pearl necklace that Dave had given her on her twentieth birthday. She'd set off her outfit with a little black straw hat festooned with flowers. Her white gloves lay on the table beside her.

They feasted on Luigi's largesse of veal parmesan with the just the right sprinkle of mozzarella on top and a fettuccini rich with extra cheeses and spices. They drank the wine and planned their future together.

When it was time to leave, Dave reached for his wallet, but Luigi waved him off saying, "You good boy, Davey. I no taka da money from you today."

"No! No! Luigi! I want to pay for this!" Dave insisted, but Luigi flatly refused. "Put back to your pockets, Davey," Luigi chided, "or you get me mad." He grinned, his gold front tooth glinting in the candlelight from the table. Luigi walked with them to the door. Taking Dave aside, he kissed his fingers to his lips the way that Italian gentlemen do. "She's a flower, Davey!" he murmured waving his hand in Thelma's direction.

The two lovers strolled home, hand in hand under a sky bursting with stars and promise.

The next morning, Dave left early for the Heart O'Gold Collection Agency. Mr. Flint looked up as Dave walked into his office.

"Right!" Flint growled. "I've got just the job for you this morning, Bellemore. The folks over at Honest Abe's Used Car lot want us to collect some overdue payments from a Lucien LaBranche. He lives on the other side of town on Union Street. Here's the address." He handed Dave a slip of paper.

"Squeeze the bastard till he squirts out cash," Flint instructed. "Whatever it takes, do it. Just get the money he owes Abe if you have to beat it out of him! He's a real loser."

Dave got the message, but he had no intention of using force on anybody. He'd had enough of that to last him a lifetime.

Dave spent a lot of time trying to find the address. He walked up and down Union Street staring at house numbers. None of the numbers matched the one Flint had given him. He was becoming more and more frustrated. He finally gave up and ducked into a small deli.

"Excuse me," he said to the clerk. "Can you tell me where this house is? I've been up and down this street ten times and I'm damned if I can find the number."

"Sure," replied the clerk. "Let's see." He took the paper from Dave.

"Yeah, I know that sonofabitch LaBranche. Owes me money. He and his girlfriend live next door, upstairs. You'll have to go around to the back alley. Bang on the door hard so they can hear you. They fight like cats and dogs. Make a hell of a racket yelling at each other."

"Hey!" he blurted out as Dave turned to walk away. "Do you have an appointment with Mae?" He winked at Dave jabbing him with his elbow. Dave shook his head and wondered why he would need an appointment with her.

Behind the deli Dave found the right door. The green paint was peeling and it was full of splinters. It looked like it had been savagely kicked over the years with heavy boots on desperate feet.

He could hear voices shouting inside but no one answered his knock. When all was quiet, he tried again. He picked up a rock he found on the ground beside the piles of stinking garbage and pounded on the door. Someone came running down the stairs, and the door squeaked open. Dave came face to face with a short, wisp of a man with oily black hair and dark, furtive eyes. He glared at Dave.

"Yeah, wha d'ya want?" he growled in a heavy French accent. His pencil-thin moustache quivered as he spoke.

Dave held out his hand. "Mr. LaBranche, I'm Dave Bellemore. I represent the Heart O'Gold Collection Agency and…"

"C'mon up, loverboy!" A woman's voice called out from the head of the stairs. Dave looked up. A slovenly woman of around forty stood at the top, clutching a soiled cotton housecoat trumpeting a burst of orange poppies. It barely covered her ample hips and sagging breasts. A red polka-dot bandana was tied around her head. Several lumpy curlers underneath made the scarf bulge out like a small sack of potatoes. A stiff fringe of hennaed frizz on her forehead poked out from under it.

"Shut yer trap, Mae!" Lucien shouted up at her. "It's just anudder goon collectin' for dat bastard Flint." He squinted suspiciously at Dave.

"Let the poor bugger up, Lucien," Mae yelled. "Don't keep him standin' there with his arse hangin' out!"

Lucien stepped aside as Dave moved toward the stairs with halting steps. What the hell have I got myself into, he wondered.

"We ain't got no money today," Mae simpered as Dave reached the top. "But come back next week after the American holiday." Business was always brisk on that holiday, and if Mae was lucky, for a day or two after.

"Or maybe you'd like a little thrill yerself. Step into the bedroom here." As she spoke her wide grin revealed several missing teeth. She gestured to an unmade bed inside the open bedroom door. "Mebbe we can make a deal, and have a good time, too." She covered her mouth with both hands, and flung herself on the bed that creaked and groaned under her weight.

Dave shuddered but kept his poise despite his feelings of revulsion.

"No thanks, Mae. Some other time maybe." And that would be a cold day in hell, he thought. He turned to leave, cursing Flint under his breath.

But Dave wasn't going to get away so fast. Lucien grabbed him by the arm in vice-like grip.

"Whoa, Mr. Big-SHOT! If Mae don't strike yer fancy, come wit' me and I show youse someting better." He steered Dave into an adjoining room.

"Eh, bien!" Lucien shot him a toothy grin. "Look, my fren'!" He waved his arm inside the room. "Magnifique, non?"

Dave's eyes bulged. The room was filled with racks of men's suits. There were dozens of them in every colour and size imaginable.

"Take yer pick," Lucien went on. "Anyting you like, der, no charge. A little off de h'arm and de coff, and yer one big fancy gent. A real Beau Brumm-ell, non?"

Dave was dumfounded. It was just like Saul Ginsberg's store. The suits were new and had their original price tags. Lucien was selling them off cheap, but a free choice was Dave's.

While he was surveying this unexpected windfall and debating the ethics of helping himself to a badly needed new suit, he could hear loud banging and cursing out on the stairs. Suddenly, the door flew open, and two uniformed policemen burst into the apartment. Dave bolted out of the room. Lucien was hot on his heels slamming the door behind them. In an instant one of the policemen jerked it open.

"Well, well," he exclaimed. "What have we got here? It looks like we've got you this time, Lucien."

"Wha' da 'ell!" Lucien roared at the two officers.

"Get dressed," the tall officer barked at Mae who was cowering behind Dave. "You're all coming down to the station."

Mae scurried into the bedroom, her bare feet slapping the floor. She threw on some clothes. Handcuffs were clamped on Lucien and on a protesting Dave. He tried to explain what he was doing there, but the police weren't interested. He'd been caught in a room full of stolen suits and that was enough for them.

"But I'm from the Heart O'Gold Collection Agency," Dave insisted. "You don't want me. I don't know anything about this!"

"Well, we happen to think you might, buddy," the cop growled. "So get down them stairs with them other two crooks." And he marched the sorry looking trio down the steps and into a waiting paddy-wagon.

Out of the corner of his eye, Dave caught sight of old Mr. Gates, who lived in the same apartment building as Dave and Thelma. He and the friendly old man had often talked together, trading stories about the two wars, The Great War of Mr. Gates' time, and Dave's more recent action in World War II. Gates was gawking at the procession, and shaking his head in disbelief when he recognized Dave shackled like a fugitive from a chain gang and the police pushing him into the back of the paddy-wagon.

As the wagon drove off, Gates hustled home as fast as his old legs would carry him. "Thelma, Thelma!" He pounded on her apartment door. "Open up!" he shouted.

Thelma jerked open the door. "What on earth is the matter, Mr. Gates! Come in. Calm down. What's happened?" Gates shuffled into the room out of breath.

"I just saw Dave!" he spluttered. "Over on Union Street. I was getting some sausages…"

"Never mind that! What about Dave? What's happened to him?"

"He was coming out of an apartment behind the deli on Union Street. He was with two other people, a man and a woman. Two policemen were with them. I can't believe it! Dave! It can't be him, I thought! But sure enough, it was Dave all right! And they were all handcuffed together. The police put them in the paddy wagon. You'd better get down to the police station, Thelma! I'll come with you!" Gates wouldn't miss this for anything.

"What in heaven's name was he doing over there!" Thelma reached for her coat and purse. "C'mon. Let's go."

~~

Thelma marched up to the desk at the police station. "What's going on here!" she demanded. "Dave Bellemore's my husband. Why have you arrested him?"

"We caught him in a roomful of stolen merchandise in Lucien LaBranche's apartment. We think he could be part of a ring of thieves from Montreal we've been investigating."

"No! Are you crazy! He wouldn't do that!" Thelma shouted. "You've got the wrong person! He's just back from the war, for God's sake! He just started a new job today!" She paused, her heart pounding. "The Heart O'Gold Collection Agency! He must've been out collecting for them! Where's a phone? I have to call his boss."

Shortly after Thelma's frantic call, Flint barged into the police station. He stormed up to the desk where Thelma and Mr. Gates were standing.

"What the hell's going on here?" he demanded.

"And who might you be?" the officer asked Flint.

"I'm Arnold Flint. I'm the Manager of the Heart O' Gold Collection Agency," Flint roared. "Dave Bellemore is my employee. He was at LaBranche's under my direction. Whatever LaBranche is up to is no concern of ours and I'll thank you to release Mr. Bellemore immediately." Flint banged his fist on the desk.

"I'll vouch for him, too" Gates piped up. "He's my neighbour and a good friend."

The policeman studied the two men, weighing their words. Satisfied that they were telling the truth, he said, "Wait here, I'll bring him out."

Thelma watched him disappear through the door.

She took a deep breath to calm herself.

When Dave walked into the room, she ran to him, hugging him. Dave looked down at her with a sheepish grin.

"You're free to go," the policeman growled at Dave. "But we may need you as a witness later, so don't leave town." He waved some papers in the air dismissing them.

Dave put his arm around Thelma as they left the police station together.

"What's it like in there, Dave?" Thelma asked, wrinkling her nose as if she'd suddenly come upon a bad smell.

There was a mischievous twinkle in Dave's eye. "Well, honey, there's a battalion of cockroaches in there that won't get to see the sunrise in the morning!"

Paula's Journey

Cal sat reading on his verandah on a warm summer afternoon. Two years ago he'd given up his taxi business in Toronto, and had retired to the little town of Tamarack with his wife, Carmen, and their daughter Anna.

They'd never regretted moving north to Tamarack and had soon adapted to the pleasures of living in a small community. They'd come here for a quieter life and a safe place to raise their seventeen-year-old daughter who'd made friends right away with all the young people in the village.

Suddenly Cal had a feeling that someone was watching him. He looked up from his newspaper and saw a thin middle-aged woman with faded red hair staring at him from across the street. As soon as he saw the woman's red hair, he felt a lurching fear. There was something familiar about her. She just stood there, looking at him. Surely not, he thought, after all these years. The nagging feeling stayed with him as he got up and went into the house.

Carmen was busy in the kitchen. She was always doing something that couldn't wait. He heard Anna skipping down the stairs. She was dressed for the beach, her bathing suit and towel over her arm.

"Swimming again?" he asked. Carmen looked up from the oven where she was sliding in a casserole for their dinner.

"Be careful down there, dear" she cautioned. "And don't be too long. Supper will be ready at five, as usual."

"I'll drive you down to the beach," Cal said. He was thinking if that woman was still across the street, he didn't want her to see Anna.

"Oh, thanks, Daddy. I'm late and the girls will be waiting for me."

As Cal backed the car down the driveway he was relieved to see that the woman had left.

~~

When the Vietnam war ended in 1975, Cal was still a young man and just out of the army. At first he couldn't find any suitable employment in Toronto, so he took his discharge pay, bought a taxicab and went into business for himself. One afternoon as he was cruising along Yonge Street, he spotted a young woman wearing sunglasses standing on the curb. Her auburn hair gleamed in the sunlight. She was trying to flag down a taxi as she juggled a large gym bag in her arms.

Cal pulled up to the curb, jumped out and opened the door for her. He always considered it part of his job to help his passengers, and the extra effort often paid off in good tips.

"Help you with your bag, Miss?" Cal reached out his hand.

"No, no! I'll keep it with me. I can manage, thanks." Her voice was strained. She clutched the bag to her chest and climbed awkwardly into the back seat.

Cal closed the door behind her. Something in her voice and manner puzzled him. He wasn't often curious about his passengers, but this one gave him an odd feeling. She seemed edgy and upset. He slid behind the wheel.

"Where to, Miss?" He glanced in the rear view mirror. The bag was on the seat beside her. She caught his eye in the mirror and almost too quickly said, "It's just a gift for my mother," as if she felt a need to explain. "Take me to the Memorial Hospital and please hurry! My father is very sick."

Cal pulled away tramping on the accelerator. Didn't she just say the gift was for her mother? Well, keep your nose out of it, Cal, he told himself. Just get going.

It was a short run to the hospital. Traffic was light and in a few minutes he pulled up to the entrance. The woman leaned over the seat, shoved some bills at him and jumped out onto the sidewalk. In a minute she had disappeared inside the hospital.

"She's in a helluva hurry," Cal muttered. He counted the money. "A five buck tip! Not bad." He looked up but she was gone. He shifted gears and pulled away, slowly cruising along the street

Suddenly, he heard a kind of mewing sound. Like a cat. Sometimes they got in under the hood for warmth. There was another faint whimper. This time he sensed it was coming from behind him. He could feel the hairs rising on the back of his neck. He pulled over to the curb and got out. In the back on the floor he saw the gym bag.

"Damn," he swore, "she forgot her bloody bag!" He reached over to pick it up and froze in mid-stretch. It was moving and whimpering! His heart started to pound. Gingerly he lifted the bag up onto the seat. It was partly open. He slowly pulled the zipper down all the way. A baby's curious blue eyes stared up at him from a cocoon of blankets. Cal jumped back in shock.

"Oh, no," he murmured. "The dumb broad ditched her kid! No wonder she left in such a big hurry."

Drivers trapped behind him leaned on their horns. Cal put the bag on the seat beside him and pulled out into traffic. He knew there was no point in looking for the woman now. He was sure the hospital story was just a ruse and she'd likely gone out another door. He tried to think of what to do.

"Shit!" he muttered. "Why me? Why anybody?"

The baby was whimpering again, and it wasn't long before the whimpers turned to screams. Carmen will know what to do, he assured himself. He stepped on the accelerator and headed for home. "Good God! Carmen will never believe this," he said aloud.

~~

Earlier that same day, in another part of the city, Paula heard the door downstairs slam hard. She felt a shot of fear. Heavy footsteps sounded on the stairs. One, two, three, then a pause, a few more, another pause. She swore she wouldn't suffer another beating. "If he comes near me again," she whispered, "I'll kill him before he kills me!"

The apartment door flew open. Frank's bulky frame filled the doorway. He was drunk again, weaving from side to side and hanging onto the doorframe. He glared at Paula through hooded, bloodshot eyes. She knew there was going to be trouble. She backed into the kitchen. Her eyes pushed at him as if to force him back.

Frank lurched toward her, his head thrust out, his red-rimmed eyes bulging like an animal about to charge. The sight of her coat and purse on a chair sent him into a rage.

"Been out with your girlfriends again, eh? They're all filthy whores! Or was it a boyfriend this time, eh?" He spat out the words. His rasping breath filled the room. Suddenly, without warning he grabbed her by the neck. "It'd be so easy to snap your damned neck," he growled, his mottled face inches from hers. His huge fist shot out and struck her a glancing blow on the cheek. She cried out. Frank loosened his grip and staggered back. He lurched toward her again with both fists up. One blow landed below her left eye leaving an ugly red welt. Another jab to her stomach brought Paula to her knees, her breath sucked out.

"One of these days I'm gonna' finish you off once and for all," he muttered standing over her his foot poised in the air.

"Frank! No, no!" she rasped, cowering on the floor. "Stop, stop! You're hurting me!"

"Shut up, shut up, bitch! Bitch! Bitch!" he roared as his heavy boot struck her in her ribs with two brutal kicks curling her half-conscious body into a ball. She lay gasping on the floor as Frank staggered off to the bedroom and collapsed on the bed, mumbling to himself.

Paula waited, too frightened to move, terrified he would come back. She was sure he would kill her this time. Panic rippled through her when she thought of little Anna asleep in her crib. After a long time she could hear Frank snoring in an alcoholic stupor. She pulled herself up. Her whole body felt like she'd been run over by a truck. She steadied herself at the counter top. A butcher knife lay in the sink. She held her bruised ribs with one hand, picked up the knife and crept into the bedroom. Frank lay spread-eagled on the bed.

At first she only wanted to scare him. But as she looked down at his gaping mouth drooling brown saliva and smelled his stinking breath, a terrible rage rose up in her. She had to silence the hideous sound of his breathing.

"You bastard!" she whispered. "You'll never lay a hand on me again!" She grasped the knife with all her strength and raised it high in the air. Then with both hands she slammed the blade into his chest, falling on top of him from the force of the blow. Her side was throbbing. She stared, transfixed, as his shirt became rich with blood spreading out like spilled red paint. She heard his breath expel in one last strangled gasp.

She stood for a moment, looking down at him. She put her hand over her mouth, her eyes wide with terror. "What have I done?" she gasped. The sight of the protruding knife handle was like a stunted limb sprouting from his body. She grasped the handle and, closing her eyes, she turned her head away and yanked it out as if by removing it she could restore Frank's life and undo the fateful course she'd set in motion. The knife slipped smoothly out of his body. Blood trickled from the blade and fell in ruby droplets onto the white sheet. She flung the knife to the floor. Her only thought was to get away. She bolted out of the room into Anna's bedroom.

Three-month-old Anna was whimpering sleepily. Paula wrapped her hurriedly in a blanket, picked up a stack of diapers and baby clothes and a bulky gym bag from the floor. In the kitchen she jammed three bottles of milk from the refrigerator into the bag, picked up her coat and purse from the chair and stumbled out into the hall. She sat down on the landing and arranged everything in the bag. Gently, she placed Anna on top of the soft pile, zipped it up part way, and holding the bag tightly in her arms she ran from the building. On a bench outside she took a piece of paper and pen from her purse. She scribbled a note and tucked it into Anna's blanket. She knew what she had to do. She had to get away. And without Anna. But how? "I can't take her! How can I look after her if I'm in prison! What will happen to her? Oh! What am I going to do!" she moaned. "Dear God, help me!" She hailed a cab and climbed in the open door.

~~

At the hospital Paula crossed the sidewalk, her eyes fixed on the revolving door. She pushed it. It wouldn't move. She felt weak from fright and the slicing pain in her side. Someone shoved the door from the other side and Paula stumbled out into the lobby. She stood for a moment trying to regain her balance. She focused her eyes on an overstuffed chair behind a marble pillar. She walked slowly toward it as if in a dream. Suddenly her legs turned to jelly and everything started swinging around and she just keeled over, grabbing the air, arms flailing and as blackness came over her she sank slowly to the cold marble floor in a crumpled heap. People rushed toward her.

"Call emergency!" someone shouted.

A man standing nearby removed his jacket, folded it and placed it under her head.

He noticed Paula's bruised face and swollen eye. "Tell them to bring a stretcher!" he called out. "This woman's been beaten up!"

A girl knelt down and draped her coat over Paula's inert body. Moments later two hospital attendants lifted her onto a stretcher and covered her with a blanket. The coats were returned and the stretcher was wheeled off on a gurney and into an elevator. The heavy doors closed behind them. The crowd began to move away.

Paula opened her eyes to sterile surroundings. A white curtain surrounded the bed. One by one the events of the past few hours came rushing back to grip her with a cold numbing fear. She began to shake uncontrollably.

"I've got to get out of here," she muttered as she stepped gingerly to the floor. Waves of dizziness forced her back into the bed. For a moment she lay there and tried to think. She stood up and slowly moved to the cupboard where a nurse had hung her clothes. She was alone in the room. She dressed quickly and opened the door a crack. The hall was empty and the elevator was just a short distance away. She moved along the corridor wall keeping her face averted. She prayed no one would see her or recognize her. She touched the DOWN button. Cautiously, she made her way through the lobby and out onto the street. She sat down on a bench at the nearest bus stop and opened her purse. She counted out thirty dollars and some change. She took out her bank book. Over several years she'd secretly managed to put aside a few hundred dollars for an emergency. She stood up and hailed a cab, hoping it wouldn't be the same man. It wasn't. The driver waited outside the bank, while she withdrew all but a few dollars to avoid any suspicion. She climbed back into the cab and directed the driver to the bus station.

She stood nervously in line. "And where are you going today, Miss?" the clerk at the wicket asked. Palms sweating, Paula glanced at the schedule on the wall. The first bus out was to Buffalo.

"One way to Buffalo, please," she said.

When she crossed the U.S. border she felt a little calmer. She sat back in her seat and tried to figure out what to do. She gazed through the window. She thought of Anna. Dear Anna, she begged. Can you ever forgive me? What else could I do? she asked herself. There was no hope for us. I did it for your sake, baby. But I promise I'll come back for you as soon as I can.

Since no one had approached her, she guessed that Frank's body hadn't been discovered yet. She looked around at the other passengers. She couldn't rid herself of the feeling that everyone was looking at her. She expected that at any moment the driver would stop the bus and the police would come on to arrest her.

The Buffalo bus terminal was crowded. She hurried to the ticket counter. She'd go to Florida – to Miami. From there she'd go to one of the Caribbean Islands and become invisible. But as she waited in line to buy a ticket she changed her mind about the bus and went outside and signaled for a cab.

"Take me to the train station," she instructed the driver. The train will be safer, she thought. I won't have to get off. She bought a ticket to Miami. She'd make further plans there. She counted her money. She'd have to be careful. It would have to carry her through until she could find work.

She shrank back in her seat exhausted. As the train hurtled southward, the clacking wheels lulled her, lifting her from mental turmoil to a few untroubled moments of sleep. A sudden jolt from the train awakened her with a start. She had been dreaming of Anna. She wondered what was happening to her. It's a good thing she can't understand what's happened, she anguished. Tears rolled down her cheeks. Oh! God! How will she ever forgive me for what I've done. This is not the way life was supposed to be for us!

The train clattered on, blowing its eerie whistle and pulling Paula away from a life marked by tragedy.

~~

Cal bumped into his driveway, brakes squealing. He grabbed the bag with the screeching baby inside. He ran up the steps and into the house, slamming the door. He came face to face with Carmen.

She stood in the hallway, her mouth fell open. "Dios!" She crossed herself. "Where did you get that baby, Cal? Whose is it?" With every question her voice climbed another octave.

"Calm down, honey. I'll tell you the whole story if you give me a chance!" Cal started toward her but she backed away, her dark eyes wide with alarm. He held the baby out to her. Carmen's expression faded into a gentle softness and she took the screaming child into her arms. "Shshsh," she whispered, as she rocked back and forth.

"Well, that's a start!" Cal muttered as he dug into the bag for anything to stop the baby's crying. He took out the three bottles of milk, and handed one of them to Carmen. He put the other two bottles into the refrigerator in the kitchen. Carmen sat down. She pressed the nipple into the child's mouth and the baby sucked greedily. It was quiet now and Cal told his story. Carmen stared at him over the baby's head.

"Incredible!" she burst out in Spanish. "What kind of mother would leave her baby in a cab?" Her eyes were wide, incredulous. "Cal!" she whispered. "It could be a gift from God!"

Cal slumped in his chair opposite her. How was he going to convince her that this was just a case of a mother abandoning her child. He felt her eyes burning into his. Cal had to look away. He could see she desperately wanted to believe that the child was meant for them.

The baby had drifted off to sleep. He watched as Carmen gently unfolded the blanket. There was a note tucked inside. She opened it. She looked up at Cal, a soft smile curving her lips. Cal always marveled at how easily she could flip-flop her emotions. "What is it, Carmen? What does it say?"

"Oh, Cal, honey! It's all true like I said!" Tears welled up in her eyes as she read the note. She handed it to him. Cal read it out loud. "Please take care of my daughter. I'm afraid for her life and for mine. Her name is Anna. Forgive me!"

They looked at each other for long minutes hardly daring to believe it. Finally Cal spoke.

"The police, Carm! We gotta go to the police! We have to take this baby to them or we could be accused of kidnapping! It's out of our hands now. They'll track down the mother, and that'll be the end of it."

Carmen's mouth fell open. She had that stricken look, the kind that Cal couldn't fight.

"Oh, Cal," she murmured. "If only we could keep her. And who would know?" She looked down at the little sleeping face. She sighed. "It's all I ever wanted!" Her eyes implored her husband to make it happen. Cal had always found it hard to resist that wistful look.

~~

At the outbreak of the Vietnam war, Cal, a Canadian, had volunteered in the American Army. His training began in Texas where he'd met Carmen. They'd fallen in love and were married before Cal left for duty in Vietnam. When he'd finally returned, he and Carmen had packed up their belongings and moved to Toronto. Carmen had pressed Cal for a home and children. A real family. Years of pinching and saving and living in cramped apartments enabled them to save enough for a down payment on a small house. But they remained childless. They'd consulted many doctors, but they all said the same thing. Cal would never be able to father a child. He'd become sterile from the chemicals the army had used in the war. It was devastating news for them. Carmen's vision of a house full of children faded away. But that had been years ago and their life together had been happy despite the absence of children.

As he looked at Carmen's stricken face, Cal felt himself relenting. "We'll keep her with us overnight," he said, "but tomorrow morning first thing we've got to go to the police." Carmen was crestfallen.

"Carmen, honey, you know it's the right thing to do, don't you?"

Carmen nodded her head reluctantly.

"I know, Cal. I don't want any trouble." She stood up and carried Anna to their bedroom. She laid her on the bed while she changed her diaper. As she took out some fresh clothes from the bag, she was thinking how healthy she was. "Someone loved you very much, little Anna," she whispered.

She emptied out one of the bureau drawers, lined it with a soft comforter, and made a little bed for Anna. Cal brought two chairs from the kitchen and placed the makeshift bed on the chairs.

"There!" Carmen said. "She'll be cozy and warm in there. If she wakes in the night, I'll give her a bottle and there's one more left for the morning." They left Anna sleeping peacefully.

Cal and Carmen sat at the kitchen table finishing a hastily prepared meal. Over coffee, Carmen related her feelings to Cal.

"I know this is not very kind, honey, but I hope they never find her mother and we can adopt her. What do you say, Cal? Could we do that?"

"We'll see, Carmen, we'll see tomorrow." He stacked the dirty dishes in the sink and they went to bed. Anna slept through the night, but Cal and Carmen slept very little.

In the morning Carmen bathed little Anna and dressed her in the clothes from the gym bag. As she cuddled the baby she wondered what terrible circumstances had driven her mother to abandon her. The last bottle of milk went down noisily as Anna stared at Carmen with large inquisitive eyes.

~~

Cal backed out of the driveway. Carmen held Anna in her arms. They drove in silence. Carmen was weepy. Her tears fell on Anna's blanket.

At the police station they were escorted into a small room. They sat opposite an officer who listened while Cal told his story. He could see the couple were upset as he explained what was their only option.

"First, Mr. Woods, we'll have to notify the proper authorities. And that would be the Children's Aid Society. They'll hold custody of the child until the mother is found. And we'll begin working on that right away."

"But we want to adopt her!" Carmen interrupted. "That is, if you can't find her mother," she added in a quiet voice.

Cal broke in. "What's the time limit for finding the mother? Can we start adoption procedures now?"

"If after three months we still haven't located the mother, I believe you can start the paper work. But you'll have to talk with the social workers at Children's Aid. They'll be able to fill you in with all the details. Our first priority is to find the mother. In the meantime, a suitable foster family will be arranged until we can locate her mother."

"But we can do that, officer!" Carmen broke in. "Let us take her home with us!"

"First the social worker, Mrs. Woods. Let's hear what she has to say."

Weeks went by. The police searched across Canada and into the border States, but were unable to find Paula. When the three-month search ended, Cal and Carmen brought home little Anna, their adopted daughter.

The years passed. Anna grew up into a loving and caring young woman. Cal and Carmen felt nothing could destroy their happiness.

~~

In the shadow of the trees the red-haired woman watched the three girls romping in the water. She smiled to herself. How young and innocent they were! She kept her eyes on them as they lay on their blankets drying themselves in the sun. She stayed hidden when they picked up their towels and clothes strewn on the sand and started to leave.

"I've got to go," Anna said to the girls rubbing her auburn hair with a towel. "Dad likes us all at the supper table together." She laughed adding, "You'd think I was going to run away or something!"

~~

Carmen was serving supper. Anna looked at Cal. "You know what, Dad?" she asked.

"No, what honey?" he answered smiling at her.

"Well, when we were down at the beach, there was a woman standing there at the edge of the trees. She was just standing there and watching us as though she knew us or something. It was really spooky."

"What did she look like, Anna?" Carmen spoke up.

"She was about your age, Mom, and she was thin and had reddish hair. I wonder what she wanted?"

"I have no idea, Anna." Carmen looked at Cal. He'd told her about the red-haired woman he'd seen and of his suspicions. Her eyes told him the moment they had dreaded for years had come.

That night as they lay in bed, Carmen looked at Cal beside her, half asleep. She was worried. She shook his arm to awaken him.

"What are we going to do, Cal? Do you think she could be Anna's mother? After all these years?"

"I don't know, honey. It could be anyone, but I'll try to find out something tomorrow." He thought for a minute. "I have an idea. Why don't you take Anna on the train to Toronto tomorrow. You could do some shopping or go to the theatre. If the woman is her mother, I don't want her coming here before we have a chance to talk to Anna."

"That's a good idea. We could get the noon train and come back tomorrow night. Anna will like that. I'll tell her in the morning." She leaned over and kissed him. "Good night," she murmured. Cal grunted, sleep overtaking him.

Anna was excited when Carmen suggested the trip at breakfast the next morning.

"Oh, Mom!" she exclaimed. "I'd really love that! Shopping and the theatre! Wait till I tell the girls!" She jumped up from the table.

"There isn't time for that, Anna," Carmen said quickly. "We'll plan the day while we get ourselves ready. The train leaves at noon. We can have an early lunch before we leave."

Anna bounded up the stairs and into her room. She dove into her closet for something to wear. Cal nodded at Carmen as if to say, well, that gives us some breathing space.

Cal saw them off and returned home. He sat down on the verandah with his newspaper and waited. After about an hour, he saw her. She was walking slowly looking at him from across the street. Cal got up from his chair. He crossed the street and approached her.

"Is there something you wanted, ma'am?" he asked politely. "I noticed you yesterday watching my house."

The woman looked at him and in a trembling voice asked, "Are you Cal Woods?"

"Yes, I am," Cal replied. "And you are…?"

"My name is Paula Rogers." She paused. "I can't believe I've actually found you. I've been looking for you for two years." Her eyes filled with tears and she blurted out, "I'm the mother of the baby you found in your cab seventeen years ago. I've been trying to find her, and I think I saw her down at the beach yesterday swimming with some friends. I'm sure that was my little Anna. The one with the red hair."

Cal nodded slowly. It was as he suspected.

"Yes," he said, "but she's our little Anna now. My wife and I adopted her." He paused. "Where did you go? Why didn't you come back for her?"

"There's so much to tell. Can we go somewhere?"

"Why don't we go across to our house? We can talk there. My wife and Anna are spending the day in Toronto."

There was an uncomfortable moment of silence when they first sat down at the kitchen table. Cal offered Paula coffee.

"Thanks, Mr. Woods. I'd like some."

Paula began her story in a halting voice. "I never came back for Anna, Mr. Woods, because I couldn't. It was all over the papers. Frank Rogers? Do you remember? His body was found in an apartment on Argyle Street?"

Cal vaguely remembered the newspaper article about the trial, and the search for the child. He'd wondered about Anna, but he didn't want to get involved and maybe risk losing his little girl.

"Frank was my husband." Paula nodded. "I killed him after years of abuse. I just couldn't take it any more. He'd given me a terrible beating that day. He tried to kill me. I was afraid he would hurt Anna." She looked at Cal for a long minute. "I didn't want to leave her in your cab, Mr. Woods. I'm so sorry, but I didn't know what else to do. I know I did a terrible thing. I'll never be able to forgive myself for leaving my baby." Paula burst into tears. She fumbled for a handkerchief in her purse. Cal handed her some tissues. She wiped her eyes and went on.

"I went to Miami. I was hoping to get work and come back for her after it all died down, but within four months the police found me and arrested me. I was so naïve. They brought me back to Toronto where I was tried and convicted of murder. I was given a life sentence but was paroled after ten years. But I had to serve another five years for abandoning my baby. When I got out I started looking for you. I spent two years talking to every cab driver in

Toronto. And then I finally met someone who knew you. His name was George Powell." Cal nodded his head.

"He told me that you'd adopted a baby. He got your address from the company's records, but you'd retired and moved to Tamarack. So I came up here to see if it was my Anna you'd adopted." Paula had been talking for an hour.

Cal hesitated. "Yes," he said. "Anna was the baby in my cab." He cleared his throat. "Mrs. Rogers, what exactly is it you want from us?"

"Nothing, Mr. Woods. Nothing at all. I don't want to cause any harm to you or your family. I'd only like her to know who I am and why I left her. If Anna wants to meet me, I'll be at the Tamarack Hotel. If not, well, I'll just have to live with that somehow." She wiped a tear from her cheek and stood up. "I promise you I'll not try to see her on my own."

Cal saw Paula to the door. He was sorry for her. But he was anxious, too, when he thought of telling all this to Carmen and Anna. Anna didn't know that she was adopted. He and Carmen hadn't thought it was necessary to tell her. Now they had to tell her. He hoped that at seventeen, she was mature enough to understand.

Later when he'd met their train, Carmen whispered, "Did you find out anything, Cal? Did you see her?"

"Later, Carmen," he murmured in her ear. "How was your trip, Anna? Did you have a good time?"

"It was great! Mom and I shopped, then we had tea in a restaurant, and after that we went to see Phantom of the Opera. It was so wonderful, Dad. You've got to see it!"

"Well, right now, let's just go home." Cal said with a grin.

At home Anna and her mother told Cal all about their trip. Later in her room, Anna put away her new clothes and soon was sound asleep.

Carmen's impatience had been growing ever since she stepped off the train. And now she couldn't contain herself any longer. "Tell me what happened, Cal! Did you find out anything?"

"Yes, and you aren't going to like it, Carmen."

Her eyes widened. "What is it?" she whispered hoarsely.

"She's Anna's birth mother all right!" Cal exclaimed. "She was back watching the house this afternoon. I was on the verandah and saw her across the street. I went over and asked her what she wanted. She came here and told me everything." Cal repeated Paula's story to Carmen.

"She doesn't want to interfere in our lives. She'd like to talk to Anna, but says she'll live with whatever Anna decides." Cal stopped and stared uncertainly at Carmen.

Carmen was distraught. "How can we tell Anna all this? She's just a young girl!"

"Tomorrow, Carmen. We'll do it tomorrow, together. But we'll only tell her that she's adopted and that the woman she saw yesterday is her birth mother. The rest of the story will be Paula's to tell."

The next morning Anna sat quietly listening to her father. It was the most fantastic story she'd ever heard. But it frightened her. Questions were whirling around in her head. "You knew all this seventeen years ago and you never told me? Why? If this woman is my mother, who was my father?" She looked at Carmen and Cal, the only family she had ever known.

The three sat at the table in silence. Cal and Carmen waited in fear, not knowing what Anna would do.

"No!" Anna suddenly shouted. "Tell her to go away. I don't want to see her...ever! You're my mother and father! I don't want anyone else!"

Cal and Carmen stared at her. Love and compassion filled their hearts.

Cal reached over and took Anna's hands in his. "I'm so sorry, sweetheart. We should have told you this long ago, but your mother didn't want to and I let it ride. What would it prove, anyway? I saw nothing but hurt for you, Anna. But before you hear anything else, I'm telling you that I'll always be your father and Carmen will always be your mother. And you, Anna darling, will always be our daughter." His voice broke.

Carmen stared at Anna. "Please, Anna," she whispered, "don't ever leave us!"

Anna slumped in her chair. "I would never do that, Mom," she sobbed.

But every day, Anna's curiosity grew stronger. After a week of debating with herself, she decided to meet with Paula.

"I've decided to meet her," she said one morning at breakfast. "Will you arrange it for me, Dad? And I'd like to see her alone at the hotel. I hope you and Mom won't be hurt, but I think it would be best. I don't know how I'll react when I see her." She looked at Cal with questioning eyes.

"Of course, Anna. I'll arrange it." Carmen nodded in agreement, her heart breaking.

Cal called Paula at the hotel. When he asked about a convenient time, she couldn't hold back her excitement.

"Oh! As soon as possible, Mr. Woods!" she cried.

~~

Anna tapped timidly on the door. Paula took a deep breath. She stood for a moment in the doorway gazing at her daughter.

"Anna, Anna," she whispered. "Please come in. I've waited so long. I thought I'd lost you forever." Her voice broke.

Anna stared at Paula. She looked for some likeness. There was no mistaking the red hair.

They sat together on the bed. Paula's heart was pounding. "I don't know how much your father's told you. But I want to tell you everything. I want to try to make up for the terrible thing I did to you."

Anna spoke for the first time. "Dad told me a few days ago that I was adopted. And that you were my real mother and you'd come here to find me. But that was all. He said whatever else there was to tell was up to you." She stared at Paula. She didn't feel any connection to her, but she was desperate to know more.

"I wondered if I should come to see you," Anna went on. "I didn't know what to do. Carmen and Cal are my parents. That I know for sure. And it will never be anything else. But I also want to know why you left me the way you did. And I want to know about my father." She looked questioningly at Paula.

"I'll tell you everything, Anna dear. You have a right to know." Paula told the story again - how she feared for Anna's safety and her own. As she talked she paused often to wipe away her tears.

"I have no excuses, Anna. It was so wrong of me to leave you. I've regretted that every day of my life." She paused. "At first my only thought was to get away with you. I never planned to leave you behind, but I knew if I was caught, you would be in the middle of the whole mess, and I wanted a better life than that for you. That's when I wrote the note and tucked it in your blanket. I took a desperate chance. But now I'm so relieved to know that you've had warm, loving parents and a stable life, something I couldn't give you. We've both been very lucky." Paula's eyes shone as she looked at her daughter. "I've always loved you, Anna. There hasn't been a day that I haven't thought about you." Her eyes filled with tears and she began to cry.

Anna felt her anxiety fading. She put her arms around Paula and they held each other, their tears mingling. Paula couldn't remember ever having felt such happiness.

"You're part of my life now," Anna murmured. "And I don't want to lose you either. Should I call you Paula?"

"Yes, I would like that, Anna dear. Carmen has been your mother for seventeen years and she'll always be so. I want to meet her to thank her and assure her that I'll never do anything to come between you." Anna held Paula's hands "Let's go home now," she murmured. "Mom and Dad will be waiting for us."

The Life of Granny Coombes

This is a telling of the time when I was ten and living with my family in Tamarack. Our home was a two-story yellow house by the railroad tracks at the south end of the village. It was the "Watkins house." My mother would often refer to it saying, "When we lived in that house of Watkins's out by the tracks…"

It was nearing Christmas and my young sister Beth and I went about our days as schoolgirls in a state of heightened expectation as we waited for Christmas day and the holidays and the gifts on Christmas morning. We'd decorated a big pine tree in the sitting room with coloured balls, lights and tinsel and every day another package would appear under it. Beth and I had a small tree up in our bedroom. A baby spruce that we'd set up on a table and decorated with cardboard cutouts we'd coloured with crayons. Mother added a few red and green balls and tinsel left over from the big tree downstairs. When we showed our handsome little tree to our Grandmother she said, "Hmph! Two trees! You girls are just mollycoddled." It was the first time we'd heard the word. We didn't know what it meant but we knew it wasn't anything good.

Christmas morning was cold but the sun was shining and the snow sparkled on the trees. Beth and I rushed from our freezing bedroom down the stairs into the warmth of the kitchen. We washed in a basin of warm water scooped from the small reservoir at the side of the wood stove, and dressed ourselves in our heavy coats and boots ready to collect our Gran from her house and bring her down the road to spend the day with us. It wasn't so much us bringing her as she was bringing us, her steps were so quick and our legs were so short. We had to run to keep up with her.

When we got home and she removed her coat and hat in the hall we saw that she was wearing the "infamous" dress. It was a black crepe and smelled of a mixture of mothballs and lavender perfume. But now the offensive appendage that had adorned the neck of it was gone, replaced with an ecru lace collar and matching cuffs on the sleeves. It was her Sunday-going-to-church dress. Mother had helped her pick it out at Colette's Specialty Shoppe in the village. Gran never liked it from the day she brought it home.

"There's something wrong with the neck of it," she'd complained, tugging savagely at the collar. She took it to a friend who did dressmaking charging her to "do something with it." The collar was removed and the dressmaker had sewn a long tab in its place. It had a bulbous tip on the end. When it was ready Beth and I went to get it. Well! Gran took one look at it and exploded.

"Did you ever see the likes of this! Saints preserve us! It looks like the thing on the front of a man!" Mother and my two aunts who were visiting at the time, burst out laughing. I, of course was only ten and had no idea why they were laughing.

There was always a package for Gran under the tree from her "New York" daughter. Mother watched as she opened the box and lifted out a pink satin bed jacket trimmed with marabou that had been dyed to match.

"Now where in the world would I ever wear a get-up like this?" Gran snorted as she folded it back into the tissue paper never to see the light of day again. It would join the layers of woolen bloomers and matching vests, nightgowns, slips and other undergarments that she was saving for special occasions. No one could guess what those occasions might be or when they'd ever occur.

"Land sakes! You should be wearing some of these things," our mother had said looking at the stockpile languishing in the dresser drawer. "It's been cold these December days and not likely to get any warmer in January."

"Uh-huh," Gran would mutter and change the subject.

I often wondered what would my aunt would have thought if she'd known that the fruits of her jostling and elbowing in the press of Christmas shoppers at Macy's on her search for something "special" for her mother up in the "frozen Canadian north" had for years been stuffed in a drawer to become nourishment for the moths. In later life I wondered if Gran had never worn the gifts because she'd never approved of her daughter marrying "that Irish Yankee of the funny religion." Even so, on Christmas Day there was always a phone call from New York when my mother and my grandmother would exchange shouted greetings with my aunt and uncle.

Christmas passed and one cold January afternoon as Beth and I walked home from school the snow creaking under our galoshes, we paused to play in the belly-high snowdrifts along the sidewalk. We always stopped in at Gran's house to check on her since our grandfather had died and she now lived alone.

"Would you split a bit of kindling for the morning, Melissa?" Gran asked me.

"OK, Gran," I answered. I headed to the woodshed, Beth following. I took down the little hatchet from the wall where it hung between two nails and began chopping at a block of wood from a pile scattered on the floor. As I cut, Beth gathered the sticks in her arms and carried them to the kitchen, dumping them in the woodbox behind the stove.

After a half-hour of chopping and gathering, Gran called out, "You've got enough now, girls. Come and wash up and come to the table."

We sat in the kitchen while she set out big sugar cookies on a plate and poured out tall glasses of milk for us. I always liked her milk jug. It was one my grandfather had bought in the local hardware store. The handle was in the shape of a cat.

The cookies were still warm from the oven. We waited until Gran passed the plate before we took one because it was "polite."

Gran's big marmalade tomcat, Maximilian (Max for short), raised himself up stretching his body out like an elastic band, his jaws wide in a needle-toothed yawn. I held out a cookie crumb and he licked it with his tongue that felt like sandpaper on my palm. He waited for a moment but saw I had turned away so he curled up at my feet in watchful readiness.

Gran always asked us about school. Our education was very important to her. She'd never gone beyond the sixth grade. Her family had moved up from Brockville when she was twelve and her mother needed her at home to help care for her little brother. John was the middle of seven children and had been born with "the palsy." He could neither speak nor walk but his brain worked just as well as anyone else's. Gran spent a lot of time with little John and could always interpret his grunts and shouts when he wanted something. When he was three years old he died of pneumonia. My grandmother always said a "labour of love had been lifted from her shoulders."

Gran lived alone after my grandfather died in 1935. My only memory of him was of the big copper pennies he gave Beth and me when we'd recite the books of the Old Testament for him with no mistakes. Beth always made mistakes because she was so young but he gave her the pennies anyway. In the evenings my grandparents seldom missed listening to "Amos and Andy." My grandfather sat by their little radio in the kitchen while Gran washed up the supper dishes. It never occurred to them that the show might be demeaning to another race of people. They would chuckle at the banter among Amos, Andy and Sapphire. The Methodist traditions were strong in my grandparents and they were especially sensitive to its pressures. They didn't know the meaning of the word racist.

Our Grandfather was not handy with tools and there was never enough money to hire anyone to do the necessary home repairs. So each year the house sagged a little more in a progressive state of decay. There was an old garage on the property that leaned precariously from the ravages of time and weather. It contained a few rusty tools, but it's main purpose was for storing chicken feed and stacks of "The Family Herald" that grandfather had saved thinking they might come in handy someday. This accumulation of paper was the source of terminal frustration for my grandmother. Grandfather liked to note the weather predictions in his little black book and he would compare them daily to the temperatures announced on the radio. When he died, his six surviving children came home for his funeral. They'd stayed on for a few days and collaborated with Gran on the destruction of the derelict garage. An agreement was reached that they would have a bonfire. People from the village came out to watch and broke into spontaneous applause as the building went up in flames and charred bits of The Family Herald rained down on them. Uncle Ben said it was like Chinese New Years!

Sometimes our cousins from Rumbling Rapids would come up by train and stay with Gran while their parents shopped for groceries in Tamarack. They were an unruly bunch of four boys. The youngest, Nipper, was always a cut-up. One day he got rummaging around in Gran's bedroom while she was out feeding the chickens. He got all dressed up in her bloomers and cardigan. The sleeves hung down over his hands. He put on a pair of her thick eyeglasses (Gran was severely short-sighted) that made him look owl-eyed. In her dresser drawer he found a set of false teeth and he jammed the uppers into his mouth. He came out clomping across the kitchen linoleum in her Sunday shoes and with the false teeth stuck out over his bottom lip. We howled with laughter at the sight of him until Gran came in to see what was going on. She took one look at Nipper, grabbed her broom and chased him through the house whacking him across his bum and shouting, "Take those things off, you little heathen! And put those teeth back where you found them. They belonged to your grandfather!" Nipper had felt the rough edge of her tongue that day. When our grandfather died, Gran had said, "I want to keep a little something of him with me," so she'd slipped his teeth from his mouth before the burial. They were the only intimate part of him that she could keep.

One notable summer after Grandfather had died, our New York relatives came to visit. They had two boys close in age to Beth and me. They talked funny and sometimes nobody knew what they were saying. It was like a foreign language to Gran. As if they'd dropped in from another planet. We teased them and mimicked them and fought with them non-stop. Some days it was the War of 1812 all over again! When they left, my father set to work to repair the screen door that had been kicked and punched into bulges and holes when our aunt had locked us out because we were so noisy. A few days after they'd left and life settled back to the usual routine, Gran was checking the ice in the icebox. To her surprise she found three brown bottles of Labatt's ale nestled around the melting ice. Being of the strict Methodist faith, alcohol was never found within smelling distance of my grandparents' home.

"Now where in the world did those come from?" she muttered and promptly poured their contents down the sink. Her dilemma was where to dispose of the bottles before anyone saw them. She waited until dark and quietly placed them in her next-door neighbour's garbage bin.

One day, when Beth and I did our usual call-in from school, we were horrified to find Gran lying on the woodshed floor at the bottom of the steps from the pantry. She'd been there for hours unable to move. She'd tried to bring in wood for the stove and had stumbled and fallen over the clutter on the floor. Her hair was full of wood chips and her knuckles were scraped and bleeding. We stood frozen staring at her. We didn't know what to do. Gran was conscious and shouting orders to us from the woodshed floor. I put a pillow under her head and covered her thin body with a blanket and squatted down beside her while Beth ran home to get help. Soon an ambulance came and she was whisked away to the hospital in the next town. She'd broken her hip in the fall. A week later the ambulance brought her back to our house. Mother nursed her in our dining room where a makeshift bedroom had been set up. Beth and I took turns fetching for her. Gran needed constant care now so we moved out of the yellow "house of Watkins" and up the road into Gran's house. She'd signed it over to my parents. It was the house my grandfather had built for her and where my mother had grown up. As a result of our move, my father fell heir to the many repairs that had been ignored over the years. His first order of the day was to be rid of all the chickens and demolish the chicken coop. He said they weren't worth the bother and they could starve to death before he'd waste any money on them. (Actually, he couldn't bring himself to kill them.) Emmett Miller was delighted to get them for his butcher shop especially when they didn't cost him a penny.

On summer afternoons Gran would sit on the front verandah in a big black leather chair. My father had bolted casters on the legs so it could be rolled easily out to the verandah. People passing by stopped to talk with her. She'd lived in the village nearly all of her life and knew everyone both living and in the cemetery. All of her seven children had been born in this house.

Gran lived with us for six or seven years until the day we had to move several hundred miles away from Tamarack. The war was at its peak and my father was transferred to an area where military protection was crucial. This meant moving all of us including our Gran. It wasn't long before old age, her crumbling hip and the trauma of leaving her beloved village took its toll and within a year she began to fade.

All these memories began to surface as I sat in my grandmother's hospital room listening to her laboured breathing and watching life slowly drift from her frail body. Her gray hair loosed from its pins, was spread out over the stark pillow. She was so shrunken it seemed as if there was nothing under the sheet. I touched her hand. It still held the warmth of life but there was a smell of death in the room. I was swamped by feelings of guilt. Guilt for not being more thoughtful of her during all the years she was a part of my life. Guilt for not comforting her when she seemed so lonely after our move. For not realizing how abandoned she must have felt moving to a strange city where she had no friends.

And how much she had missed everyone back in the village. She'd never complained but patiently accepted life as it came to her. How I wish I'd taken the time to listen when she talked about her life. Now it's too late. But all the memories and regrets still haunt me.

Web of Power

Thump, thump, thump. The pounding on the floor above brought Lena abruptly down to earth. "Lord, give me strength," she muttered. She'd been daydreaming about Cliff again. Lately, just about anything made her think of him. But the racket from Maudie's bedroom interrupted her thoughts. Lena rolled her eyes upward. "The impatience of the woman!"

She put a bowl of steaming porridge on the breakfast tray. Maybe Maudie would like this nice crusty roll instead of toast this morning. Lena hoped it might put her sister in a better mood. She filled a cup with fresh coffee. She added a sugar bowl and a jug of cream to the tray. She wrapped two spoons and a knife in a white linen napkin, added a jam-pot and paused to check everything over. Nothing was forgotten.

Thump, thump, thump.

"I'm coming, Maudie!" Lena shouted. She picked up the tray and moved toward the stairs. She could take only one step at a time because the tray was so heavy, and she had to take care not to spill any coffee in the saucer. Maudie hated that.

Upstairs, Maudie gripped her cane in her pudgy fingers and was about to rap out another summons, when Lena appeared in the doorway, pausing to catch her breath.

It was stuffy and hot in the bedroom. The low ceiling always trapped the heat, and the small room was warming with the hot breath of the coming day. The walls were papered with big red roses that seemed to intensify the clutter. Every inch was covered with fading portraits of deceased family members, old Currier and Ives prints and other yellowing scenes in ornate brass frames. The room was crowded with heavy furniture. A faded tapestry-covered footstool sat on the floor beside the bed. Sometimes children, who came with their mothers to visit with Maudie, would hide the little stool under the bed when nobody was looking. They would crouch giggling in the hall outside her door to see if she could find it, muffling their laughter with hands cupped over their mouths.

There were books and magazines everywhere. Old newspapers, outdated copies of National Geographic, Life Magazines and even some Agatha Christie mysteries, all in a jumble with romance novels littering the floor. It looked as if Maudie had just flung the whole mess off her bed and onto the floor. She had more books than anyone in the village – books of poetry and large books of prints, all stacked every which way in a bookcase leaning against the wall. Cardboard boxes full of old newspapers and magazines were piled behind the door. She never threw anything away.

Maudie lay sprawled on top of the bedclothes. She was not quite four feet tall. Her short thick body and stumpy arms and legs shifted restlessly on the rumpled sheets. Her gray frizzy hair lay on the pillow like Medusa's snakes.

When she was born, the doctors had cautioned her parents to be kind to her. "She will not live longer than two years, probably less," they'd told the stunned couple. Their advice to "be kind" was taken to the extreme by her family, with the result that after all these years, her sister was still catering to Maudie's every whim.

Maudie always knew she was different. Even as a young child she recognized the curious stares of strangers that made her skin prickle all over. In time, she grew used to their gawking, and ignored them by protecting herself with a hard shell of hostility. Her parents had tried in vain to prepare her for a life of disability, but she fought them and said they were wrong and that her short stumpy body and oversized head were just a passing phase, and that she'd soon grow into a tall and pretty girl like her sisters.

"Dwarfs are just in fairy tales!" she scoffed. "They aren't real people!" Her parents watched sadly as every day, she would shinny up the kitchen doorjamb, and hang from the frame until her stubby little fingers grew numb, hoping to stretch herself into an average size. It pained her father to see her hanging there with such determination, and he would gently lift her down to the floor.

From an early age, she learned to use her body both as a shield from the taunts of children and the stares of strangers, and as a weapon to gain control over her life as well as over the lives of her family. This morning her patience with Lena was wearing thin.

As Lena entered the room with the tray, Maudie heaved herself up against the pillows and smoothed the sheet over her lap. Lena leaned over the bed and carefully set down the tray. Then she crossed the room and lifted the blind, flooding the room with the morning sun. She raised the window to let in the cool morning air. The lace curtains billowed out in the breeze. She took a deep breath, smelling the freshness of the air and letting the warm sun bathe her face.

"Well," Maudie spluttered. "I nearly gave up on you, AND my breakfast. What on earth kept you?"

Lena turned toward her and tried to ignore Maudie's scowling face. "How are you this morning, Maudie? Did you sleep well?" She watched Maudie's stubby fingers pick up the roll.

"What's this?" Maudie snarled holding up the roll. "It's as stale as yesterday's news!" she grumbled. "It's as hard as a rock, Lena! You can take it right back to the kitchen. I can't eat that! Imagine! Paying out good money for dried out bread!"

She hurled the roll at Lena. It struck her on the cheek and fell to the floor. Lena turned away. Tears stung her eyes. She was trembling with anger. Maudie didn't notice.

"It's NOT stale!" Lena's voice was low and shook with rage. "The crust is supposed to be hard. It's very soft and fresh inside. Ed Graham said they were just made this morning. I bought them especially for our breakfast today. Just try it, Maudie! It's very tasty with a bit of butter and jam!"

"You eat it then," Maudie hissed, "and bring me some toast. Do you think you could manage that, Lena?" She settled back against the pillows, her short arms folded across her chest. Her thick lips were puckered in a childish pout.

Lena struggled not to give in to tears. She knew that was what Maudie wanted. She looked out of the window.

"Another lovely day," she said, feeling the warm sun through the open window. "You really should come down to the porch and enjoy some sunshine and fresh air. You've been cooped up in this stuffy little room for days, Maudie!"

"I'll decide that when I'm good and ready, and not before. I don't need an engraved invitation in MY OWN HOUSE!" Maudie flung the words at Lena.

The house did belong to Maudie. Mr. and Mrs. Nelson, the parents of the five children, Maud, Minnie, Bridget, Thomas and Lena, had left the family home to their disabled daughter after their deaths. They'd agreed that life would be difficult for Maudie and they'd wanted to be sure she'd always have a home for as long as she lived.

Local gossips said that the sisters gave up their lives caring for "poor little Maudie" to fulfill a death-bed promise made to their widowed mother. The parish priest, Father Cleary, who was attending the old lady at the time of her death, was said to have been a witness to it all as the sisters gathered around the sick bed. Of course their brother, Thomas, wasn't bothered by any of this and went on with his own life.

One after the other, Lena's two older sisters died, first Minnie, then Bridget, having devoted their lives to Maudie. Now it was up to Lena to carry on the promise.

At a young age Maudie had discovered that the vow her sisters had made to their dying mother gave her some power over them, and she played on it unsparingly to get her way. Whenever she was confronted by a rebelling sister, she'd cruelly remind her of the promise made before Father Cleary, who'd kept his eye on the family over the years, making sure the vow he'd witnessed was being fulfilled. In those days, the clergy held a powerful influence over their parishioners. Father Cleary's involvement in the lives of the Nelson family and his authority in the village, were enough to keep the sisters faithful to their promise. Not only was the priest a constant reminder, but there was always that crushing guilt the sisters felt at being whole, while Maudie was trapped in an unforgiving body.

When Bridget had died after years with Maudie, it was thought the poor woman succumbed from a heart condition from overwork and stress trying to please her irascible sister. With both Minnie and Bridget gone, Lena had resigned her job as secretary to the Controller of General Motors in nearby Oshawa. She'd moved into the house that now belonged to Maudie. Then it became Lena's turn to take over the job of caring for Maudie. Nobody had expected Maudie to outlive two of her sisters.

At that time, Lena was already engaged to be married to Cliff Bates. The two had met at a church social during one of her holidays in Tamarack. Cliff owned a thriving hardware business in the village. He'd lost his wife to cancer and he'd never remarried. He and Lena began seeing each other regularly, and their friendship had blossomed into a loving relationship. Both were in their mid forties by then, and they'd made plans to marry soon, and settle down in Tamarack where they'd grown up together. Lena had returned to Tamarack from Oshawa, with the idea that she and Cliff would marry and live with Maudie, and that she would continue caring for her sister with Cliff at her side.

When confronted with this situation, Cliff was adamant in his refusal to live "under Maudie's thumb." He knew all about her temper tantrums and scheming ways from back when they were all children at school together. He'd watched Maudie manipulate her parents and her sisters for years, and he was determined that she wasn't going to do the same to Lena or to him.

They'd talked and talked but Lena could see no way out of the dilemma. In the end, she'd broken off their engagement. When they'd parted for the last time, Cliff held her in his arms and brushed the tears from her cheeks. He spoke softly, his voice trembling. "Lena, Lena, don't do this! I love you so much, and I know you love me. Can't you see that Maudie will just use you as a doormat, and you'll end up just like Min and Bridget. Please, please, dear, don't throw away our lives together, now that we…" Tears rolled down his cheeks, as he pleaded with her.

Lena hadn't wanted to lose Cliff. She'd loved him dearly and still did. But the seeds of guilt had been deeply planted. She'd thought of her sisters, Minnie and Bridget, both faithfully keeping their promises year after year. Lena had resigned herself to what she saw as her fate. She knew she could never abandon Maudie. She'd pulled away from Cliff's embrace. Her tears spilled over as she whispered, "I'm so sorry, Cliff, but can't you see how hopeless it is? It's my duty to look after her as I promised."

Cliff had had no answer. He just walked slowly away.

Lena stumbled up the steps and into the house. She'd thrown herself down on her bed. Utter despair had engulfed her.

Maudie had pretended not to notice Lena's grief. She'd watched furtively from the sidelines, as Lena's happiness slipped away. She'd had moments of fear when she could see herself living with strangers who wouldn't be so willing to do her bidding. Or worse still, she could be living in an old folks' home.

~~

Five years have passed since Lena and Cliff parted, and Lena is now fifty years old. Maudie is seventy. This morning, after the fuss with Maudie over the breakfast roll, Lena returned to the kitchen and sat at the table, her head in her hands. Tears trickled between her fingers and splashed onto the blue checked tablecloth. "This won't do," she scolded herself. She dried her eyes on her apron and reached for a loaf of bread in the breadbox. She dropped two slices into the toaster. Her thoughts drifted back to Cliff. Somehow she couldn't stop thinking about him.

"He was so right," she sighed. "I should have married him, and let Maudie sort out her own life. It's all my fault, keeping this foolish promise, giving up my life and with precious little thanks for it." Lena had never felt so alone, so empty.

The toast popped up. Lena buttered it, picked up the plate and trudged back up the stairs to Maudie.

"That's more like it!" Maudie snapped as she smoothed a blob of strawberry jam on the toast. Lena watched as Maudie munched the toast. A wave of despair settled over Lena. She fought it for she knew these feelings could take over her life. And then where would I be? she asked herself. Old and miserable, like Maudie.

"Let's have a game of scrabble after breakfast." Maudie stuffed the last crust into her mouth. A toast crumb bobbed up and down on her lip as she spoke.

"Well, if you really want to," Lena answered reluctantly. She hated playing with Maudie, who always had to win or there was no living with her for the rest of the day. But there was no living with her anyway, if Lena were to refuse.

Lena set the empty plate aside on the bedside table and found the scrabble box amid all the clutter on the floor. It was just where Maudie had thrown it after their last game. She pulled a discarded breadboard from under the bed to hold the game on Maudie's lap. They set out the letter tiles on the wood frames. Maudie pressed her lips together in concentration. The wooden tiles clicked in the silence.

"I've got a word!" Lena exclaimed. Maudie leaned over squinting at the board.

"That's not a word!" she scoffed. "There are two P's in 'opposite'. That's too many letters, dummy!"

Lena groaned. She never could remember if the word had one or two P's. She looked up catching Maudie's mocking grin.

"It must be lonely being right all the time, Maudie," she said, removing the misspelled word with a flourish.

There was a lull while they pored over the game. Maudie, deep in concentration, twisted her hair around her fingers, a habit she'd never outgrown from childhood.

Suddenly, Lena began to sing as she pondered the game.

"Amazing Grace

How sweet the sound

That saved a wretch like me!

La la lalalala la.." Lena loved that hymn. Her thin soprano quavered in a pious warble. She rattled the tiles as she sang.

Maudie jerked off her glasses, and rolled her eyes upward.

"Will you please stop that caterwauling in my ear!" Maudie shouted.

"Oh, I'm sorry, Maudie. I just like to sing when I'm concentrating!"

"Well, I don't want to hear it! Just play, for goodness sake!" Maudie fixed her watery, gray eyes on her sister as she twirled her hair.

"Yes, yes, all right!" Lena put some letters on her board. "Oh!" she cried. "Look! I've got one! Forlorn!" She spelled it out. "F-O-R-L-O-R-N!"

"I know how to spell it," Maudie retorted. She leaned over to check it out. "Well, congratulations!" she sneered. "You deserve an Oscar for that one!"

Lena ignored her. Maudie took her turn. She stared at the letters. She picked one up, looked at it, then put it down. She took another. She rearranged them. Then she took them off the board. The minutes ticked by.

"Headway! That's a good word!" Maudie cried out. "It's something we don't seem to be achieving in this game." She sat back with a smug and lofty smile.

Lena didn't answer. She was tired of Maudie's shrill voice and her constant criticisms, the pettiness that never ended. With a sigh she searched her tiles for another word.

"Momma would've liked this game. Don't you think so, Lena?" Maudie prattled.

"No! She would not! She couldn't read or write!"

"That's not true! Not a single word of it! She was an intelligent woman, and a courageous one too! Why, I remember when she used to paddle Poppa's canoe from the farm to the Chippewa camp across the river to deliver babies. How many times did she take food and clothing over there? Don't you remember? Those poor people were nearly starving to death." Maudie's gaze drifted off. "Momma was a real saint if ever I saw one!" The thought held her imagination. "She should be in the Hall of Fame," she added.

Lena snorted. "Well, I never!" she exclaimed. "Hall of Fame, indeed! More likely Ripley's Believe It or Not!"

Maudie scowled as her stubby fingers impatiently rattled the tiles. She couldn't think, her anger was so intense. How dare Lena scorn their mother's good deeds! The minutes dragged on.

"For God's sake, Maudie, are we playing this game or not?" Lena had reached the end of her patience.

"It's your turn DUMBBELL!" Maudie shouted. "And there's no call for that kind of language, Madam Lena!" Maudie shot back. "You never in all your life heard that kind of talk at home. Poppa never approved of swearing! He was a very refined gentleman!" Her eyes narrowed, and she pursed her lips into a row of wrinkles.

"Well," Lena smirked, "I guess he never played scrabble with you!"

Maudie banged her fist down on the board, sending the tiles flying across the bed.

"That's it!" she shouted. "I've had enough of you. I'm going to watch television." She grabbed the TV remote from the bedside table and clicked on "As The World Turns."

Lena put away the scrabble game and escaped down the stairs. "She wouldn't know if the world was turning or if it suddenly came to a grinding halt," she snorted, shaking her head. Despite all their bickering, Lena still had feelings of compassion for Maudie. She understood the reasons behind Maudie's make-believe. She knew that it was only an attempt to make her dull life interesting, even if she had to rely on a little exaggeration from time to time.

Over the years, Maudie had pieced together her own version of life on the farm, and her telling of it became more and more far-fetched as she added new tidbits to the stories. All of the made-up tales were her way of holding someone's attention, for Maudie was lonely. Her comfortable home, her books and her television could not dispel her frustrations. She knew there was more to life than what she had. She felt shut out, with nothing to contribute as she watched her school chums grow up, marry and start families, and she began to pull back from them. She retreated to her bedroom, where she would keep to herself, with only an occasional visit from some of the women of the village who felt sorry for her. Sometimes she would come downstairs for a visit with Lena's friends when they came to call. And very often they would cut short their visits because of Maudie. She never saw that her hostility only isolated her more from the very people she wanted to have as friends.

~~

The doorbell rang. Rita, their sister-in-law, stood on the front steps, her arms loaded down with newspapers and magazines.

"I've just been to the Post Office," she said as Lena opened the door. "Norma said you hadn't been in for days, and she couldn't squeeze another thing into your mailbox. Is everything all right, Lena?" she inquired. She held out a handful of letters and papers.

"Oh, yes, everything's fine, thank you, Rita. How good of you to bring all this. Come in, come in." Lena reached for the bundle of papers, setting them on the wicker table. "Maudie signs up for too much of this rubbish. She never reads the half of it! And she doesn't share it with me! Keeps it all in her room. Says it's all too deep for me! Can you imagine the cheek of her!"

"How is the Grand Duchess today?" Rita asked, laughing.

"Oh, she's the same as ever. You know, she always has a burr up her bustle!" She made a wry face. Rita tossed her head back with a chuckle.

"Come, sit down." I'll put the kettle on for tea," Lena said as she started toward the kitchen.

Rita had been married to Thomas Nelson for thirty years. They'd never been blessed with children. Lena had wondered, but she'd never asked. Maudie wondered, too, and she made no bones about asking. But Rita would just purse her lips and change the subject, figuring it was none of Maudie's business.

Tom had died of a heart attack last year, and Rita lived alone in a small apartment at the end of the street. She and Lena had been best friends when they were both young girls at school, and they'd maintained their friendship over the years.

Rita's eyes filled with compassion as she watched Lena leave the room. She thought back to the years before Bridget died, when Lena was working in Oshawa. She'd had a very good job there. She was such a pretty girl, too. Rita smiled remembering how desperate Cliff Bates was to marry her. But Maudie stepped in and put the kibosh on that.

She looked up as Lena came back with a tray of tea and cakes. Strands of gray hair fell loose from the coil at her neck. A drawn look was etched on her face. She looked older than her fifty years. Why she's as thin as a rail, Rita thought. A good puff of wind would blow her away.

Lena set down the tray, and poured the tea. She passed a plate of brownies to Rita.

"These are lovely and fresh from the bakery this morning, Rita," she said. "Maudie didn't like the rolls I bought for breakfast. But I think she'll like these. Poppa always said she had a sweet tooth."

Lena's pampering of Maudie annoyed Rita, but she said nothing. They sipped their tea in silence. It was a comfortable silence between old friends.

Suddenly, Rita looked up. "Lena! Listen! Isn't that Maudie coming down the stairs?"

Lena raised her head. "Why, yes, she is!" she exclaimed. "She must have heard your voice, Rita!"

They both turned toward the doorway as Maudie waddled into the room. She wriggled her top-heavy body up into a chair, and settled herself in a nest of pillows. Her short legs were covered in a pair of white stockings, and they stuck out off the end of the chair like two sawed-off logs. Black patent-leather Mary Jane shoes were strapped to her swollen feet. Her puffy ankles bulged over the sides like rising dough. In her rush to get down the stairs, she had thrown on an old green skirt, and topped it with a frilly blouse of shiny red satin. The buttons were done up all wrong, leaving the top two open. She hadn't taken the time to comb her stiff hair either. A gleaming silver hair clip in the shape of a bird clung to the side of her frizzy head in an attempt to control her unruly mop of hair.

Why, she looks like something out of Snow White, Rita thought as she stared at Maudie. She could hardly resist an impulse to laugh.

"Well, here you are then, Maudie! How are you?" she asked. "You certainly seem chipper today, coming down the stairs. And you managed it all on your own, too."

Maudie detected the slight sarcasm in Rita's voice, but she ignored it. They both knew the reason behind it. She glared at Rita. Don't think I don't know what you're up to Miss Rita, she thought to herself. I know you've been trying to separate Lena and me for years. But your schemes won't work. She'll never leave me!

The two women had never liked each other. Rita refused to put up with Maudie's high-handedness. Even when they were little girls, Rita resisted Maudie's bossy airs, and this irked Maudie as much now as it did then.

Maudie peered at Rita through her thick lenses.

"Oh, I'm well enough, Rita" she whined. "A little worn out from all the hustle and bustle around here, though." Behind her glasses, her myopic eyes were huge and reproachful, as she glanced at Lena.

Lena's jaw dropped in astonishment. "The only 'hustle and bustle' around here is what you stir up, Maudie," she replied, her eyebrows arched.

Maudie lifted her eyes defiantly, and was about to fling back a nasty retort, when Rita stepped in to prevent a dispute. Maudie's mouth remained contorted with her unspoken words.

Rita rushed on. "I was thinking the other day about the farm your mother and father had years ago down by the lake. It was so lovely there in summer with the big oak trees shading the farmhouse. And your mother's flower gardens! Weren't they something! The splashes of colour were like a painting when you looked up from the gate. Tom and I always loved to go down there. It was so peaceful!" She closed her eyes and inhaled deeply. "I can almost smell the perfume of the lilac bushes along the path," she sighed.

"It was just like an artist's palette," Lena joined in. She was so pleased with the image she repeated it. "Like an artist's palette. Do you mind, Maudie, before the farm was sold?"

"Of course I remember!" Maudie scoffed. "Hampton-Rowe Hall. I named the place. Don't you remember the stationery I had engraved with HRH in gold letters encircling our family crest? It was so elegant! We were the envy of the whole village!"

Rita grimaced. HRH, indeed! Her Royal Highness! How appropriate, Rita thought. She was sure the crest was something out of a book somewhere. Maudie was always searching for a link to the British aristocracy, and with a name like Nelson, she was sure there had to be a connection somewhere. Maybe even to Horatio himself! Maudie's pretentious stationery had been a source of ridicule among the townspeople and an embarrassment to her father. When the little farm was sold, the fancy note-paper was tossed into the cookstove with the kindling for a morning fire. Hampton-Rowe Hall was just another small farm gripped in an endless struggle to survive. It's grandeur existed only in Maudie's mind.

"I remember one time before Poppa sold the farm, a man came down and wanted to buy it. Poppa wouldn't let him in the house." Lena laughed as she told it. "Shoved him right off the porch, he did. Kept yelling, 'Get out! Get off my land!' The poor fellow ran off, scared out of his wits!"

The three women laughed together. For a few minutes they were silent, remembering the day and the old man's anger.

"It was the shotgun that did it," Lena piped up. It came out quickly, as though she hadn't intended to say it.

Maudie lurched forward. Her thick fingers were poised on the chair arms, as if she might propel herself into the air at any moment. Her eyes turned hard. "What shotgun?" she spat out.

"Poppa's shotgun!" Lena exclaimed. "He fired a few blasts in the air to scare the man off. Don't you remember?"

"He did no such thing," Maudie blustered. "He never owned a shotgun in his life! And even if he did, he'd never fire it at anyone! He was not a violent man! You're mistaken, Lena. Oh yes, mistaken!" Her face was flushed and she squeezed her lips shut.

But Lena persisted. "Then how do you explain all the rabbits and venison we ate back then? They didn't just jump into the pots by themselves, Maudie!"

Rita bowed her head to hide a smile.

"We never ate those gamey things," Maudie spluttered. "We always had the best cuts of meat from the butcher! And we had our own chickens!" She emphasized the words with a thump of her cane. "Your brain is becoming addled, Lena," she said in a superior tone.

"Well!" Lena shot back, "I would rather be a little 'addled' than live in your dream world! Your imagination has run away with you again, Maudie!"

Rita rose to leave. She set her teacup on the tray. Lena's eyes pleaded with her to stay. "Oh, don't leave so soon, Rita, she begged. "You just got here!"

"Yes, I really must go," Rita said. "I'm making peach jam and must get going on it before the peaches spoil." She hadn't even bought the peaches yet, but she'd had quite enough of Maudie's wrangling.

Lena walked her to the door.

"Do come back soon, Rita," she murmured. "So we can have a nice visit by ourselves." She kept her voice low, out of Maudie's earshot.

"Oh, Lena!" Rita whispered, "she's absolutely..." she searched for a word. "POISON!" she exploded. Lena covered her mouth lest she burst out laughing.

She watched as Rita walked away. How I envy her, she thought. So trim and smart-looking in her gray pant-suit. And that mauve scarf! It's just perfect with her silver hair. She certainly doesn't look fifty.

She looked down at her worn brown oxfords and her old, flowered housedress. She was still wearing her apron from breakfast. She shook her head remembering all the stylish clothes she'd worn when she was working. All the elegantly tailored suits and expensive shoes with purses to match. She sighed and closed the door.

Her face was tight when she returned to the living room. Maudie sat propped up in her chair looking like a Christmas ornament in her red and green get-up and the gleaming silver clip in her hair.

Lena picked up the tea tray.

"Lena! What's all that racket out front?" Maudie whined.

"Oh, it's just Timmy Bates and some children playing on the street."

"Well, go out and tell that brat to go home and take his rowdy friends with him. I can't listen to that all day!"

Lena set the tray down and went to the door. The children looked up as the door creaked open. They thought it was Maudie coming to yell at them again.

Young Timmy Bates squealed, "It's the Tasmanian Devil! Run, run!"

The gang scattered like a flock of startled birds, flapping their skinny arms and screeching, "Tasmanian Devil! Tasmanian Devil!" as they disappeared from sight.

Lena grinned. Why, the cheeky little monkey! He was so like his Uncle Cliff. Cliff had always been a relentless tease, and Lena could remember hating him when they were children. But that had changed as they both grew older and fell in love.

She closed the door and turned back to Maudie.

"They're all gone," she said.

"Thank goodness." Maudie grumbled. "Nowadays, children don't know how to behave! I declare, I don't know what this generation is coming to. Why don't their parents take them in hand? They're all too pampered and have no respect for anyone or anything. Discipline has gone completely by the boards!" She railed on as Lena took the tea tray to the kitchen.

~~

The following morning as Lena was sweeping off the front steps she heard Maudie screeching. She rushed into the house, flung the broom in a corner, and ran up the stairs. Maudie was lying on the floor beside her bed in a twisted heap.

"Help me up, Lena," she shrieked. "I think I've broken something."

"Ohhh! she screamed, as she struggled to sit up.

"Don't try to move, Maudie. I'll call an ambulance. You'll have to go to the hospital. Lie still, now. I'll be right back." She covered her with a blanket. Maudie's wailing followed Lena down the stairs.

In ten minutes the ambulance was at the door. Two attendants lifted Maudie onto a stretcher and carried her out like Cleopatra on her chariot. She continued to screech hysterically with pain and fright. The two men tried to calm her, but she only screamed louder. Lena climbed into the ambulance to comfort her.

At the hospital, Maudie was whisked away. Lena sat in the waiting room. Her thoughts were all on Maudie. What'll happen to her? she wondered. How long will she be in here? She'll surely hate it. They won't be catering to her every whim here.

After an hour or so she saw their family doctor, Dr. Mills, coming through the swinging doors.

"How is she?" Lena asked, rising to her feet.

"Well," Dr. Mills began slowly. "I'm sorry to say, Lena, that Maudie's right hip is broken. And it looks like a pretty nasty break. There isn't much we can do for her right now except to make her as comfortable as possible. We've given her a sedative to calm her down. She's sleeping now. Surgery may be a possibility but we'll know more in a day or two, after I see some X-Rays. Right now, I suggest you go home, get some sleep and we'll see what tomorrow brings."

Lena picked up her coat from the chair. She turned back to Dr. Mills. He took her hands in his. "Good night, my dear," he said. "I'll talk to you tomorrow when I can tell you more. And try not to worry, Lena."

Lena nodded and thanked him. At the reception desk she phoned for a taxi to take her home.

Maudie remained in the hospital for many weeks. The nurses were fed up with her demands. She complained to anyone who would listen. She was a nuisance to the staff who were doing their best to care for her. Lena visited her every day, loaded down with personal belongings and books that Maudie wanted, but never looked at. Lena brought food to supplement the hospital meals that Maudie called "swill for the pigs."

Now that Lena was free from her need to be at home with Maudie every day, she began to get out socially with Rita. Together they attended concerts and lectures in the church hall. They went to parties given by old friends, many of whom Lena hadn't seen for years. She joined an afternoon bridge club at Rita's insistence. Together they attended church regularly, like in the old days.

The change in Lena was dramatic. With Rita's help, she bought new clothes, and had her hair cut in the latest style. Out from under Maudie's thumb, all her old tensions were fading away.

One Sunday night, the two women were attending a lecture and slides given by a visiting African missionary in the church hall. Lena was watching people taking their seats.

Suddenly, she saw Cliff across the aisle with his brother, Roger, and little Timmy. Lena's heart leaped. It had been a long time since she had seen him, and then often only a glimpse from her porch window as he drove by. The flood of emotions she felt surprised her, and she realized that the love she felt for him was still alive. She nudged Rita.

"Look who's sitting across from us," she whispered. Rita leaned around her.

"My, my," she whispered back, "if it isn't Cliff Bates!"

Lena couldn't resist staring. Although he was now in his early fifties, Cliff still showed traces of his boyish good looks. His hair was streaked with silver, and there were a few more wrinkles on his tanned face, but she saw he was still lean and fit. He was dressed in khaki trousers, a plaid shirt and a light coloured golf jacket.

"Hmmm! He must be spending a lot of time on the golf course," Lena whispered.

"Looks like it," Rita nodded. A plot was taking root in her head. Wonderful! This is a perfect time to get these two together again. Her thoughts were racing ahead.

When the program ended, Rita steered a reluctant Lena to Cliff and Roger who were talking together, coffee cups in hand. They hadn't noticed Rita and Lena sitting on the other side, in the middle of the row.

"Well, well," Rita chirped as they came toward the two men. "I'm surprised to see you here, Cliff, and you too, Roger! It's been a long time, hasn't it?"

Cliff's eyes were riveted on Lena. "Lena, Lena," he said softly. "How are you? You look wonderful!" The admiration in his voice and in his eyes as he searched her face erased any thought that he'd forgotten her.

"I'm fine, Cliff. Just fine," Lena stammered. She grasped at words. "What a nice surprise!"

"Where's Timmy?" Rita suddenly asked. Roger looked around him.

"Oh, he's around somewhere with his friends. They're likely stuffing themselves with cookies and pop. I'd better round him up before he makes himself sick, or his mother will kill me! Gloria's out to a choir meeting tonight." He winked at Rita.

"I'll come with you," Rita spoke up. She avoided looking at Lena, and she and Roger strolled away leaving Cliff and Lena alone. There was an uncomfortable moment of silence and then Cliff spoke up.

"I heard about Maudie's accident," he said. "Tough luck. I hope she's feeling better now."

"She's coming along slowly, thanks Cliff." Lena's head was spinning, and she could feel her cheeks burning.

"Good, good," he nodded. There was a long pause when neither of them seemed to know what to say next. Then Cliff decided it was now or never.

"Well, Lena, now that you have some time to yourself, how about joining me some night for dinner in town, just the two of us. Say, some night this week. That is, of course, if you're free. What do you say?" His eyes searched hers for an answer. But before she could answer, Rita and Roger joined them, with Timmy in tow.

They stared at the young boy in amazement. For some reason, known only to young boys and not too clear to adults, Timmy had tied his shoelaces together for a prank, and he had pulled the knots so tight, he couldn't undo them. He couldn't get the shoes off, either. The more he struggled, the tighter the knots became. His friends had laughingly left him to his own devices. When his father and Rita found him sitting on the floor, almost in tears, they tried to untangle the mess, but with no luck. An embarrassed Timmy had to hop along beside them. They all tried not to laugh, but they couldn't hold it in. Timmy had broken the ice between his Uncle Cliff and Lena.

"C'mon Sport, let's go home." Roger took Timmy by the hand, and they hopped to the door together, like two kangaroos, leaving everyone watching with amused and puzzled looks.

Cliff grinned at Rita. "I'm trying to make a date with Lena, but she's giving me the brush-off." His eyes appealed to her for support.

"Oh, go ahead, Lena," she urged, waving her hand toward Cliff. "It's time you had a little fun. Long overdue, I'd say. And look at it this way," she laughed. "It will be one less dinner you'll have to cook!" Her eyes darted from Lena to Cliff and back to Lena.

Lena felt trapped. She had no reason not to go, but she couldn't rid herself of a feeling of uneasiness. Nothing will come it, she thought. There is still Maudie. Maudie, sick and needing care now more than ever. But, she reasoned, Maudie is still in the hospital. So what harm could one dinner do? I'll do it! I'll go with him! She smiled at Cliff and Rita.

"All right, you two schemers," she agreed, laughing. "I know you're both ganging up on me!" She turned to Cliff.

"That would be very nice. Thank you, Cliff. I'd be delighted." She paused for a moment. "How about Wednesday night?"

"Wonderful. It's settled then. I'll call for you at seven Wednesday night. I'll make a reservation at the Mediterranean. The food is good, and their wines are excellent. I've been there a few times. I'm sure you'll enjoy it." He smiled his boyish smile. "See you then, Lena." He winked at Rita. "Good night, partner," he said.

Cliff strode out to the car where Roger was waiting with Timmy. He took a deep breath, and slowly exhaled. He was glad he hadn't let the opportunity pass by, and he danced a little jig as he approached the car. He slid into the seat beside Roger.

"I take it you had some success in there," he said to Cliff, laughing at his brother's antics.

"Yep!" Cliff said with a grin.

"Good stuff!" Roger said smiling, as he headed the car toward home. Timmy, in the back, struggled with his shoelaces.

Lena and Rita walked home together, arms linked. A steady stream of doubts flowed from Lena. "I don't think this was such a good idea, Rita," she said. "I still care for Cliff, but I'm afraid of getting hurt again. And I don't want to hurt him either."

"Don't be silly, Lena," Rita said. "It's only dinner," she laughed. "It's just two old friends getting together again."

"I suppose you're right. I guess I'm worrying about nothing."

The days flew by. Soon it was Wednesday. It was 6:00 P.M. Lena had been fretting all afternoon.

"Get a hold of yourself, you silly fool!" she scolded herself as she rummaged in her closet for a suitable dress. She picked out a simple black silk sheath that flattered her figure, still slender at fifty. *I haven't worn this since my* retirement party, she mused. A double strand of pearls at her throat would be her only jewellery. Black patent pumps that had been carefully preserved in tissue paper years ago accentuated the delicate curves of her calves and her slender ankles. She'd always been blessed with beautiful skin, and a slight touch of make-up enhanced it. Her silver-gray hair was cut in a short, flattering style.

"What am I thinking of!" she fretted. "I can't do this!" Her hands shook as she reached for the telephone. But before she could pick it up, it rang. Rita was on the other end.

"I hope you weren't planning to cancel, Lena," she chided. "Anyway, it's too late for that. I just saw Cliff go into Christina's Flower Shop." She chuckled into the phone. "Have a wonderful time tonight. I'll call you tomorrow." She hung up before Lena could answer.

She heard the doorbell ringing. She zipped up her black silk sheath, slipped her feet into her patent pumps and ran down the stairs. She was nervous as she opened the door. "Come in, come in, Cliff," she said breathlessly.

"Hello Lena." He smiled as he held out a small white box.

"A white gardenia for a lovely lady." He sang it off-key to the tune of "Red Roses for a Blue Lady." Lena smiled, remembering his romantic gestures in the old days.

Cliff opened the box for her. Lena picked up the delicate flower with trembling fingers. Its sensuous perfume was like a fragile ribbon drawing them together.

"Oh, Cliff!" she exclaimed, "it's lovely! Thank you!" She breathed in the heady scent.

Cliff took the flower from her, and tried to pin it on her dress. Standing close to her, he was nervous and clumsy as he fumbled with the tiny clasp. Lena retrieved it.

"Still butterfingers!" she laughed, and went to the hall mirror. She pinned it high on her shoulder and turned to face him.

"Very nice, very nice," he murmured. His admiring look told her that he still cared.

She picked up her small beaded bag and black gloves from the sofa. Cliff held her coat.

"I guess I'm all ready!" she said, as she looked around the room to see if there was anything she had forgotten.

"Oh, my keys" she called out and picked them up from the coffee table. "I don't want to forget those, or I won't be able to get back into the house!"

"I think I still know how to jimmy a window!" Cliff was laughing.

As they rode in the car they were both silent for a few miles, feeling a little self-conscious. Lena broke the silence.

"You look like you've been golfing a lot, Cliff. You're so tanned. It suits you, too."

Cliff smiled and kept his eyes on the road. He was thinking of how he could make this reunion last. Lena chattered on.

"You know, Cliff, I didn't get out much when Maudie was at home. She needed so much attention, that I couldn't do a lot outside of the house." She glanced at Cliff. He said nothing. He eased into the highway traffic. Lena rambled on.

"There was always so much to do. I couldn't even get out to church. But Rita and Gloria have always been so good to us. Rita came in almost every day with our mail, and they both often brought casseroles for our dinner. Sometimes they would both arrive on the same day!" she laughed. "They're such great cooks. Both Maudie and I always enjoyed..."

"Stop dancing around, Lena." Cliff interrupted. "You know why we're both here." He glanced at her profile. "I've never stopped loving you, not for a moment. I never married again because I never got over you. It almost destroyed me when you left."

Lena shot him a surprised look. She hadn't expected such frankness. She took a deep breath. Since he was being so candid, she couldn't be any less.

"Oh my dear," she murmured, touching his arm. "Do you really think it was any easier for me to give you up? Do you have any idea what life has been like for me since?

Putting up with Maudie's constant complaining. Wondering if I'd made a huge mistake by turning you away? And now, here we are, right back where we started, with Maudie still in the middle!"

Cliff pulled the car off to the side of the road. He turned and took her face in his hands. "Tell me the truth, Lena. Is it too late for us? Do you feel anything at all for me? I want to hear it from your own lips."

"Cliff, I'd be lying if I said I didn't still love you." Her voice faltered. "I never forgot you. I know now it was foolish of me to tie myself to Maudie for so long, giving up my own happiness. But I made the decision, right or wrong, and now it's too late to change it. Maudie will come home sooner or later, and I'll be looking after her again. And all this will seem like a lovely dream!"

"No, Lena! No, no, no!" Cliff was adamant, as he held her in his arms. "I won't let that happen! We'll work something out. As long as I know you still love me, I swear I'll find a way for us to be together. This life you're leading isn't natural! It's long past time you started having a life of your own, and I want you to share it with me! The years are passing us by, sweetheart! Don't send me away again!" He kissed her tenderly on the lips. "Let's just enjoy what we've found again! And no talk of the past." He released her and pulled the car back onto the highway. Lena felt the old desire for him surfacing.

At the restaurant, Cliff checked their coats, and the maitre d' led them to their table. Cliff had ordered a bottle of champagne earlier, and it was waiting for them on ice. A waiter filled their glasses. Cliff's voice was soft and husky. "To you, Lena my love, and to us, and to many more happy times together."

They talked about their childhood days and growing up in Tamarack. They laughed about the teachers that they liked and those they didn't, remembering little incidents that had stayed with them over the years. Maudie seemed as far away as China.

Too soon it was time to leave. They'd spent four hours catching up after so many years of being apart. Their conversation during the evening had revealed to each other the loneliness of their solitary lives. The hours had slipped by unnoticed.

Because of the late hour, traffic was light on the drive home. Cliff glanced at Lena. She's so beautiful, he thought.

"You don't know how happy you've made me, Lena." His voice was quiet and full of emotion. Then without any warning, he pulled off the road and stopped the car. His arms closed around her as he whispered, "Let me take care of you, Lena dear. There's nothing in the world I would rather do than be with you for the rest of my life." He held her tightly as if he would never let her go. Lena's tears splashed down on his coat sleeve. She was unable to speak. He kissed the top of her head and held her away from him, his hands on her shoulders so he could look into her eyes.

"There has to be some way we can be together. I'll find a way. I promise you that, my darling!" His voice was low, his words barely audible. He grasped the steering wheel, and pulled the car back onto the highway. Lena was shaken by the strong love they still felt for each other.

"I hope so, Cliff," she whispered.

At her door, Cliff held her and kissed her tenderly. He didn't want to leave her, but the propriety of the times was observed, and they parted with promises to see each other the following day.

Lena prepared for bed. She lay in the darkness trying to piece together the events of the evening. Her thoughts were only on Cliff. So strong and confident. She would place her trust in him, and pray that he could solve their difficulties. Her mind was racing too wildly for sleep. Thoughts of spending her life with him held her imagination.

The phone rang. She reached out to the bedside table and lifted the receiver. Who could be calling at this hour, she wondered. She had a fleeting thought that Maudie may have been trying to contact her.

"Hello?" Her voice was guarded.

"I just wanted to hear your voice again, sweetheart." Cliff's voice vibrated over the wire. "Tell me, did I hear you say you loved me, or was I just dreaming?" For a moment,

Lena was speechless. Her voice caught in her throat as she murmured, "Oh, Cliff! I want you to know that tonight was very special for me. No matter what happens to us, I'll always treasure it. And yes, I do love you very much, and I always have. I'll see you tomorrow, I promise!"

Lena slowly replaced the receiver. A warm feeling of contentment washed over her and she fell into a sound sleep.

Over the days that followed, anyone who saw them together couldn't help notice that Lena and Cliff were still very much in love. Their renewed romance caused some gossip in the village, but their friends were happy for them. There were many idyllic dinners at the Mediterranean, where they had recaptured their love. Sometimes they included Roger and Gloria. Rita, too, was often a dinner companion.

~~

Later that same year, Roger and Gloria planned a two-week holiday in Florida. Timmy would remain at home with Gloria's mother, as he was in school every day. During a lunch break one day, Roger walked into Cliff's hardware store and approached his brother with a plan that he and Gloria had agreed upon. They'd hoped it would speed up the new romance between Cliff and Lena and result in their early marriage.

"How about it, Cliff?" Roger asked. "Gloria and I would like you and Lena to join us on our trip south. See if you can talk her into it. She needs to get away from Maudie and those daily treks to the hospital. She must be fed up with that routine every day. She would be good company for Gloria, too, while you and I spend some time on the golf course. What do you say?"

"Well, I sure like the idea but I don't think Lena will agree, Rog." Cliff sighed. Spending two whole weeks with Lena would be a dream come true. "She's very proper, you know, and probably wouldn't think much about unmarried couples taking trips together."

"Well marry her, for Pete's sake, and make it legal! I don't understand you two and your dilly-dallying around for so many years! You're wasting precious time, man!"

"I'll talk to her, Rog, that's all I can promise. It'd be a perfect chance to convince her that we belong together, and as you say, the sooner the better."

~~

Lena struggled up the long hill to the hospital, her arms full of books and food for Maudie. To add to her suffering with a slow-mending hip, Maudie had developed a severe case of bronchitis. Dr. Mills thought it wise to keep her under his watchful eye for a little longer.

Lena set her parcels on the night table beside Maudie's bed. She leaned over and kissed Maudie's pale cheek. "How are you feeling today, Maudie?"

Maudie gave her a woebegone look. "Oh, I don't know, Lena. I'm not in very good shape," she whined. "My hip isn't mending, and now this!" She coughed hard as if to confirm her condition. "The doctor says it will be a long time before I'll be able to walk again. If ever," she added, and brushed a tear from her cheek.

Lena was moved. She hadn't seen Maudie in tears since she was a little girl when she would cry bitterly because she couldn't understand why she was so short. She grasped Maudie's hand. "Don't worry, Maudie," she said soothingly, "you'll be as right as rain by summer, and you'll be home long before that. Listen to Dr. Mills, and do what he tells you, and I'm sure everything will turn out just fine."

Maudie half nodded in agreement. "What did you bring me to eat, Lena? I barely touched any food today," she complained. She poked around in the bags, selecting a juicy orange.

Lena peeled it for her with nervous fingers. She had to tell Maudie of her decision to join Cliff in Florida with Roger and Gloria. She knew Maudie wouldn't like it. Maudie knew Lena was seeing Cliff again, thanks to one of the local gossips who'd visited her in the hospital. Maudie had hoped to be back home by now and squelch the affair, but she was helpless to do anything about it from the hospital. She watched suspiciously as Lena shifted uneasily in her chair.

"Maudie," Lena began quietly. Her head was lowered as she peeled the fruit. "I'm going to be away for a couple of weeks, so I won't be able to..."

"Where are you going?" Maudie broke in quickly.

"Well," Lena explained nervously, "you know I've been seeing Cliff again."

"I know all about it!" Maudie shouted. "So?" An alarm bell went off in her head. What if Lena were to marry Cliff this time? What would happen to her? Where would she go? She was afraid of what lay ahead.

Lena began slowly. "Well, Roger and Gloria have asked Cliff and me to join them for a couple of weeks in Sarasota…that's in Florida, you know."

"I know that!" Maudie shouted. "Get on with it!"

"And so," Lena continued, "I've agreed to go with them."

"Are you out of your mind, woman?" Maudie roared. "You can't go travelling with a man you aren't even married to! What will people say! You know what it's like around here. It doesn't take much to get people gossiping." A fit of coughing stopped her for a few minutes. Lena opened her mouth to speak but Maudie continued.

"You have to tell Cliff Bates and that meddling brother of his that you ARE NOT GOING WITH THEM!" She struggled to sit up, pointing her finger at Lena. "It's positively indecent! I forbid it!" She fell back against the pillow gasping.

Lena was stunned at the angry outburst that flew out of Maudie's mouth. She'd expected opposition, but not this tirade.

Maudie gathered her strength and continued to berate Lena. "You're acting like the whore of Babylon! You silly fool!"

That was enough for Lena. Maudie's uncalled for abuse fuelled her determination to settle the issue once and for all. "I won't change my plans, Maudie, so you can stop wagging your finger in my face," Lena said, a slow burning anger flaring inside her. "I'll be leaving on Friday with them, and we'll all be back in two weeks." She rushed on, determined that Maudie wasn't going to spoil anything this time.

"I love Cliff, and I always have, and I will not let you or anyone else stand in our way this time and that's final! And while we're on the subject, you might as well know now that Cliff and I are planning to be married next summer, so you'd better start thinking about your future too. I'll be living with him in his house, so you won't have to worry about him being under your feet." She felt a rush of relief now that it was all out in the open. Years of frustration lifted from her shoulders.

Maudie was dumfounded. Her mouth hung open but no words came out. She stared at Lena, her eyes were wide with alarm. In all the years they'd been together, Lena had never spoken to her like this. Her world was unravelling around her, and for the first time in her life, she was powerless to change it. Her stubby fingers plucked nervously at the bedclothes.

Lena's hands were shaking as she picked up her coat and purse. At the door she turned back to Maudie. Her voice softened as she looked at Maudie's stricken face.

"I'll be back in two weeks, Maudie. It's not a long time, and then we can talk more about all this." She tried to explain her feelings. "You have to understand that I love Cliff deeply, and I want to spend the rest of my days with him. He wants this too, and we're both determined to see it happen this time. I'll call you from Florida every day."

She bent down to kiss Maudie's averted cheek. "Everything will work out, Maudie. You'll see!" She closed the door and left the hospital. Maudie sat in stunned silence, not knowing which way to turn.

The following afternoon, Maudie had an unexpected visitor. The door to her room opened and she was face to face with Cliff. Lena had told him about the argument she'd had with Maudie.

"What are YOU doing here?" Maudie shouted. "If you've come to butter me up you're wasting your time." She glared up at him.

"I've come to tell you to mind your own business, Maudie, and leave Lena and me alone. You've interfered in her life long enough. It's time she had some happiness and I intend to see that she gets it." Cliff's face was flushed.

"And just how do you plan to do that, Mister Cliff Bates?" Maudie's lips curled.

"By marrying her, of course. And if you upset her once more I'll see that you are put away in a home far from both of us. And I can guarantee that you won't see much of Lena if that happens. We'll move away from Tamarack if we have to. Anything to get away from you and your meddling in our lives. We're going to Florida together and I don't want to hear any more from you or you'll see that this is not just an idle threat!" He turned on his heel and slammed the door after him.

Maudie grabbed the books from her bed and flung them one after the other at the closed door. "I'll NEVER go into a home! NEVER! NEVER! I DON'T NEED YOU CLIFF BATES! I DON'T NEED ANYONE!" she shouted.

Maudie lay awake in bed for a long time. Cliff had influence in the community. He was a member of the Hospital Board and she feared he could do what he'd threatened. And Lena was just fool enough to let him. She could end up in an old folks' home. The thought of that terrified her.

~~

It was Lena's first trip south. She was determined to enjoy every minute of the next two weeks. The warm weather, the Gulf breezes and the beauty of the gardens were an aphrodisiac to her starved senses. She felt reborn and free after weeks of going to the hospital and catering to Maudie's wishes. The hostility between them at the time of their parting bothered Lena, but she promised herself she would make it up to Maudie when she returned home. Right now, she just wanted to bask in all the attention and love that Cliff was showering upon her. In the mornings, Roger and Cliff played golf, while the two women shopped or just sat around the pool reading and gossiping. At night, the two couples sought out the local restaurants. Later, Cliff and Lena would stroll alone on the beach and talk about their wedding plans and their future together. They were concerned about Maudie and tried to plan what could be done for her. Often they would join Roger and Gloria in their room for a nightcap before bed. Cliff and Lena had separate rooms. Cliff was too much of a gentleman to suggest any other arrangement.

It was an exciting time for them as they discovered each other again. They were continually amazed at how much they thought alike.

"We'll make a great team, Lena," Cliff happily assured her. They both yearned for the day when they could be together as husband and wife.

In the middle of the second week, Gloria and Lena went shopping and left the brothers relaxing over a scotch and water on the balcony. The ringing telephone interrupted their friendly banter. Roger disentangled himself from his lounge chair and went into the bedroom. What now? he wondered. Did the girls run out of money? He picked up the receiver.

"Hello."

"I have a call for Lena Nelson," the operator said.

"I'm Roger Bates, her fiance's brother. I'll take the call. Put it through."

"This is Dr. Mills speaking, Roger. Is Lena there?"

"No, she's out right now, Doctor. May I take the message?"

"Well, Roger, I'm afraid I have some bad news for Lena. Her sister Maudie died this morning." There was a brief pause, and the doctor went on. "She'd been suffering from a bad case of bronchitis that had developed into pneumonia. The infection progressed so rapidly we were unable to save her. I'm very sorry to have to give Lena this tragic news. I know she was devoted to her sister."

Roger was speechless.

"Are you still there?" the doctor asked.

"Yes, I'm here," Roger answered dully.

"Then, I wonder if you would be good enough to have Lena call me? She'll no doubt have some questions and perhaps I can help soften the blow."

"Yes, yes, of course, doctor. I'll do that just as soon as she comes in." Roger took down the doctor's number and hung up the phone. He turned around to see Cliff standing in the doorway.

"What's up, Rog?" Cliff asked anxiously.

"It's Maudie!" He stared at Cliff. "She died this morning. I can hardly believe it! That was Dr. Mills for Lena." They both fell silent, thinking about what this tragic news would do to Lena.

Roger gathered his thoughts. "He wants Lena to call him. Here's the number, Cliff. But how did he know where to call?"

"Lena gave the hotel number to him before we left," Cliff answered. "My God, she'll be floored by this! I know they had an argument at the hospital about our wedding." He paused. "I need to be alone with her when I tell her, and when she calls the doctor."

"Sure thing!" agreed Roger. "Take the message and go to your room. When they come, in I'll tell her you're waiting for her there."

Cliff left with heavy steps. *This will destroy her*, he thought. *Things are hard enough for us, and now this.* He shook his head and wondered what lay ahead for them.

As soon as Lena stepped into Cliff's room, she stopped short. She stared at his solemn face. "Cliff? What's the matter?" she whispered, still clutching her packages. He took the parcels from her and set them on the bed. He moved toward her.

"Lena, I'm afraid I have some terrible news." He hesitated not wanting to go on. "It's Maudie!" His voice faded as he looked into her stricken face.

"What is it? Tell me, Cliff! She's not..." She couldn't finish what was in her mind.

Cliff took her in his arms. "Maudie died this morning in the hospital, Lena." He felt her body sag against him. He pulled her close. "Dr. Mills called while you were out. He wants you to call him and he'll give you more details." He stroked her hair. "I'm so very sorry, my love. So very sorry!"

Lena clung to him. She was numb with shock. Her world had stopped. Tears sprang up and trickled down her cheeks. Cliff murmured words of comfort.

Her voice broke the silence in the room. "Oh, God," she whispered hoarsely. "We had a terrible row when I left. And now, I can't...." her words ended in a sob. She didn't know what she felt. Confusion, anger, but most of all, guilt.

She pushed away from Cliff. "I have to get home. Right away. Maudie needs me now more than ever." She started for the door. "I have to pack. Cliff, we have to check out." She was rushing around the room unable to think of what to do first.

"It's all right, Lena." He drew her close to him. "Roger is checking us out right now, and we'll leave just as soon as we're all ready. Gloria's packing their things. I'll help you get ready and you can call Dr. Mills from your room."

As they turned to leave, there was a light tap on the door. Cliff opened it. Gloria rushed by him to Lena, embracing her.

"I'm so sorry, Lena. Roger just told me. Don't worry, we'll get away from here as soon as we can. Come with me to your room. I'll help you pack."

She turned to Cliff. "Cliff, you stay here and get yourself ready. When Lena and I are finished you can pick up her bags and take them down with yours. Roger is loading our luggage in the car now."

She took Lena by the arm and they left. Cliff threw his clothes and toiletries hurriedly into his bag. He left his room to pick up Lena's suitcase sitting outside her door and he carried it with his down to the lobby. The two women sat in the car while Roger and Cliff loaded everything. Roger got in behind the wheel, Gloria beside him. Cliff and Lena sat close together in the back. They drove away leaving behind what had been a blissful holiday.

~~

Tamarack seemed far away. The trip back was quiet. The miles flew by, but the stop-over nights seemed endless. Lena was unable to sleep. The guilt she had so recently shed had returned in one great surge. She sat pale and withdrawn, hardly uttering a word during the trip. Cliff sat beside her, holding her cold, limp hands until they pulled into Tamarack three days later.

Cliff went into the house with her. Inside she turned to him and broke down, sobbing bitterly in his arms.

"It's all my fault!" she cried. "My fault! I should have been here with her. I should never have left with so much anger between us! We fought, Cliff. It was awful! The things I said! I can never take them back now, or tell her how sorry I am!" The tears kept coming as Cliff held her close.

"Shsh, shsh." Cliff tried to comfort her. "There was nothing you could have done, Lena. Even if you'd been with her. Dr. Mills assured you on the phone that it was hopeless. It all happened too fast. They couldn't do any more. Please dear, don't blame yourself. You're not responsible for Maudie's death."

"But I wasn't here with her," Lena sobbed. "She died alone, with no one to comfort her!"

"I know, I know, it's awful it happened while you were away, but you couldn't know. No one could know. Listen to me, Lena! You must understand you're not to blame. What could you have done for her?"

"She never had a life!" Lena moaned. "I cared about her, I really did, Cliff. But I never told her, and now it's too late." She stumbled into a chair and held her head in her hands. She swallowed hard, trying to control her grief. Suddenly, she jumped to her feet. "There's so much to do!"

she cried. "I don't know where to begin." She took a deep, ragged breath.

"Don't worry about any of it right now, sweetheart," Cliff answered. "Roger and I will take care of everything. Try to get some sleep. You're exhausted."

Lena stood still, staring at Cliff's worried face. Whatever would I do without him, she thought. "Thank you, Cliff," she whispered. "Give me some time to think. We're both tired and you've done so much already. I'm so grateful. I'll call you tomorrow." She stood on tiptoe and kissed him softly. Cliff hovered by the door. He didn't want to leave her, she looked so helpless. He hoped she would be able to get some rest before tomorrow.

Lena took a long time preparing for bed, dreading the silence and all the thoughts and recriminations that would burden her. Sleep was a long time coming. She wished she could turn off her mind, flick a switch and black out everything. Finally, sheer exhaustion propelled her into a night of fitful sleep.

In the middle of the night, Lena awoke in a cold and clammy sweat. Reality swept over her. All of the old smothering guilt rose up, her heart was pounding. Once again, she pushed Cliff into the background, and again, even in death, Maudie was in control. All the longings for a future with Cliff flitted away and she felt that part of her life was finished forever. Right now, her future was beyond thinking about.

For two days Lena and Cliff went through the ordeal of preparing for Maudie's burial. They met with the village priest to discuss the service. Lena did all this in a mechanical state of mind, like it was not really happening.

The sun was shining the morning of the funeral. There was a steady flow of people into the funeral home. Some who came to mourn Maudie were the same people who never sought her company when she was alive.

When everyone had left for their cars and the procession to the church, Lena and Cliff were left alone with Maudie. Lena looked down at her sister, lying so still, so peaceful. In death, Maudie's skin looked like creased paper it was so delicate. She had the serene look of the very old, and the vacant look of death. Her thick lips had taken on a bluish tinge, resembling two slices of darkened rubber. Her stunted body was hidden at last from prying eyes. Only her large head of frizzy hair, now combed into submission, and her shoulders covered in her best black dress, were visible. Lena wept quietly in the silence. Cliff pulled her close to him.

After the burial, the church hall overflowed with many of Lena's old friends and others who came out of curiosity. A luncheon had been arranged by some of the women in the village. The room buzzed around her with voices. Lena accepted their condolences quietly with Cliff at her side. She wished desperately they'd all go home.

~~

The house seemed huge and empty when Lena returned home. She refused the offer from her friends to stay with her, and also from Cliff, who really wanted to be with her. Her sorrow was one she wished to bear alone. She tried to eat a few morsels of food, but she couldn't swallow anything. She prepared to retire for night. In the doorway of Maudie's room, she stood for a long time. Then she softly closed the door. She kept to herself in the days that followed. No amount of coaxing from Rita or Cliff could dispel her feelings of regret and loss.

Sometimes in the stillness of the house, Lena thought she could hear Maudie's cane banging on the floor above. At other times, she could see her face, hear her laughter when Rita would visit, and the three women would revive old memories over a cup of tea. Her constant reminiscing kept her in isolation. She was living in the past, and couldn't face the future.

Lena continued a loving relationship with Cliff, but it was never more than that.

"I need you, Lena. I want to be with you," he pleaded. But Lena couldn't think of anything else but Maudie dying all alone.

"I know I'm being unfair to you, Cliff," she said. "Please try to understand. Maudie's death has changed everything. The way I feel now, I wouldn't be good for you. I couldn't give you the happiness you should have. It would all end in resentment toward each other, and you deserve better than that."

Cliff looked at her with sadness. "I'll never give up hope that we'll be together someday."

Lena gradually came to terms with Maudie's death. Her marriage to Cliff had been put aside, but their love for each other never faded.

~~

It was the middle of a Sunday afternoon. Cliff and Lena had returned from church service in the morning, with a promise to get together for a "nostalgic supper." Cliff was in a poetic mood as he quoted, "a loaf of bread, a jug of wine, and thee beside me, singing in the wilderness." Lena smiled. Cliff would always be a romantic.

It was a beautiful warm summer day. The sun beckoned them to the lake for their picnic. Cliff had gone home to prepare the food. Lena would supply the wine.

She searched in her closet for something casual to wear. They'd planned to go down to the place where the Nelson's old farmhouse had been. It was an empty field now, with four or five picnic tables scattered about. The old lilac bushes were still there, lining the overgrown path that led nowhere, ending abruptly in a patch of shrubbery gone wild.

Lena chose a blue flowered cotton skirt, and a short-sleeved blouse of navy blue. She picked up her white cardigan from the bed to ward off the cool lake breezes.

I'm going to enjoy this, she mused, seeing the old place again. The house had been gone for years, but the memories were still there. As she dressed, childhood remembrances began to surface, when her parents were alive, and the five children played and worked on the farm.

The chiming doorbell interrupted her thoughts. She hurried down the stairs, expecting Cliff, but when she opened the door, it was Rita who stood there. She took one look at Rita's face and knew something was wrong.

"What is it, Rita? What's happened?" She pulled her inside. "You're as white as a sheet. What's wrong?" She felt the old fear rising up again.

"Oh, Lena! I don't know how to tell you this. It's so awful." She stopped, her eyes downcast, afraid to face her. Tears trickled down her cheeks.

"Please, Rita, tell me what's happened!" Lena's voice shook.

Rita looked up. She held Lena's hands. "Lena, dear, it's Cliff," she whispered hoarsely. "He's had a heart attack. And, oh my poor girl, he's gone!" There was no way she could soften the blow. She stood still, her lips trembling as she stared at Lena.

Lena heard the words, but they didn't register in her mind. She pushed away from Rita's grip. "No! That's not true," she exclaimed. "We're going to have supper later by the lake. At the old farm." she added. "Cliff's home right now, preparing the food. It's to be a surprise, he said. What you're saying can't be true, Rita!" Her eyes begged Rita for a denial.

"Lena, Lena, please listen to me. It happened just an hour ago. He was in his kitchen fixing the food when he just keeled over! Roger found him. The ambulance came, and they took him to the hospital. But it was too late! He was gone! Oh, Lena, I'm so sorry, so very sorry!" Rita was crying softly.

Lena stared at Rita's bowed head. This can't be happening, she thought. Why, just this morning he was with me at church. He was teasing me about the big surprise he was going to prepare for our supper! How could he have died so quickly? She was unable to accept it, she was so numbed with shock.

Rita led her to the couch and they sat together. Rita was crying, clutching Lena's cold hands. Lena stared straight ahead, her body rigid in denial. They sat together in silence until Gloria came and drove them to her home. Rita and

Gloria did their best to console Lena, suffering her own private grief.

~~

At Cliff's funeral, Lena's sadness settled into a kind of tranquility. Years and years passed by in her thoughts. How many thousands of years ago was it, she asked herself, that we planned to marry. We were so much in love. Why, oh, why did I keep refusing him? He waited so long, and so patiently, but I always kept him at a distance. Her thoughts were suffocating her. "What have I done?" she whispered. In that moment all the wrong paths she had taken in her life returned to torment her.

Lena looked around the room at the faces of the many friends who came to pay their respects to her beloved Cliff. It seemed the whole village was there. This was the same room where Maudie had rested. Her thoughts went back to her sister. Poor Maudie! We were adversaries right to the end! Lena took a deep breath. Tears welled up in her eyes, and she looked at Cliff lying so still. Her thoughts shouted inside her head. Cliff! Cliff! My darling one! My only love! Why did you leave me? She gazed fondly at his handsome face. Her pensive look suddenly became one of horror. Instead of Cliff's face, she saw Maudie's image grinning back at her in triumph, as if to say, "I told you so!"

Rita saw the change in Lena's face and rushed to her side in time to catch her swaying body and take her home.

~~

It's a month after Cliff's funeral and Lena is sitting alone in her living room. The warm summer sun is streaming through the windows fanning out across the room and suspending tiny dust motes in its beams.

She is thoughtful. A folded letter lies on her lap. Lena found the letter in a bag of books she'd brought from the hospital after Maudie died. The bag had never been opened until today, when Lena decided to try to sort out all the jumble of papers and books in Maudie's closet. The letter has put her in a pensive mood. What had prompted Maudie to write it, she wondered? Had she finally realized what kind of person she really was and wanted to make amends? Or did someone change her mind for her? Lena picks the letter up and reads it again.

"Dear Lena," it says,

"Today, I'm feeling a little stronger, so I'll try to write this letter to you. It's been on my mind, since you told me of your plans to marry Cliff Bates and you left for Florida with him. Things were said and done between us that day that can't be undone. And so I've decided not to go against your wishes any longer. I've spent a lot of time thinking in here. It's such a dreary place. I often think of how Momma took care of me...and Bridget and Minnie. They were so good to me. They loved me and promised they'd never leave me. They never broke their promise. But you, Lena. Well, that's a different story. You want to leave. You want to marry that Cliff Bates. I want you to know he came to see me before you left. We had a chat. Why you want to spend the rest of your life with that man is beyond me. He's beneath us. He has no breeding. What would Momma say? What can you be thinking of? Our parents are turning in their graves. Turning in their graves! But I've had a lot of time to think here. What else is there to do? You off in Florida with that man. Me stuck here in the hospital with no family and no visitors. Well, I've decided to forgive you. Yes, I forgive you. After all, you're the youngest and the weakest of the family. You don't have the wisdom of Bridget or Minnie. If you are silly enough to want to marry that man and throw your life away, I won't stop you. I'll find someone with a brain to take care of me. Someone I can trust. Don't ever think you're indispensable. You're not. I'll get a nice, simple girl from Tamarack and I'll be just fine. So then, I give you my blessings. I hope you get what you wish for. And you know what Momma always said about wishes! Go off and marry your Cliff. And if you ever think of your poor sister, come and visit me—alone."

    Maudie.

Escaping the Net

Today was the first time Alfie Long had come to his wife's grave since he'd buried her a year ago. He hadn't planned to be here but he'd had no choice after his neighbour, Ivy Gilliam, handed him a bouquet of flowers from her garden.

"I thought you'd like to put these on Rose's grave, it being a year ago today and all," she'd said.

And so here he was, kneeling in the freshly mown grass beside Rose's tombstone. He lay the flowers on the soft mound by her head.

"Ah, Rosie, Rosie," he sighed. "We sure had a rough time, the two of us. Fifty long years and nothin' to show for it." Spoken out loud the stark words shocked him. He struggled to remember the good times. Like the fresh scent of his pajamas after Rose's Monday wash. How she would roll up his clean socks in tight little balls and arrange them neatly in his sock drawer. And the bed linen that had captured the smell of fresh air as it flapped on the clothesline. All the little things that Rose did to make his life pleasant. He tried to recall what pleasures he'd given her, but none jumped to his mind. Her round face flashed before him. She had that patient look she'd get when he'd tell her one of his worn-out jokes. Rose always gave him that weak smile even though she'd heard his stories a million times.

She didn't often smile though. She'd go days without talking to him. She wasn't angry. She just didn't have anything to say. When he closed his eyes he could see her in their kitchen in her big white apron preparing supper. He frowned when he remembered the clutter of dirty pots and pans that surrounded her when she cooked. She'd have flour up to her elbows, smudges of it on her cheeks and white patches of it all over the floor. The sight of it always made him irritable. But no matter how nasty his remarks, she'd pretend she didn't hear him and carry on with whatever little jobs she had in hand. Rose never answered back. And that angered Alfie even more. She'd never speak up for herself. He would have respected that.

He looked down at her grave. He felt nothing. How could he grieve for her when there was hardly anything he could remember about her. She'd left him with nothing, not even the ability to mourn. She'd been practically invisible.

"How did we end up together, Rosie?" he said. "We never really loved each other, did we? All those wasted years! So many wasted years!"

He remembered the night he'd proposed to her. She was only twenty, and she'd said "yes" right then with Alfie still on his knees in the family parlour. He was taken by surprise at the speed at which it had happened. And how unsure he felt after it was done. But there was no turning back for it. Fifty years! And their disastrous wedding night.

He'd never forget it. Their physical union had been a bittersweet moment. The bedsprings creaked and groaned in the darkness. When it was all over, Rose lay trembling like a wounded sparrow. She'd turned away from him sobbing into her pillow. He felt humiliated. He wanted to be far away from her.

As he knelt beside her grave now, he heard quiet laughter. He stood up and looked around. A pretty middle-aged woman stood at a nearby headstone. He ambled over to her and squinted at the inscription. "Angus Murdoch, born July 15, 1925. Died Sept. 10, 1995. Loving husband of Mary McAllister Murdoch."

"Why that's the same day my Rose died!" Alfie said, pointing to the stone. "Quite a coincidence, eh?"

"Was that yer wife you was talkin' to?" the woman asked with an amused glint in her eye. "I hope you said nicer things to her when she was alive!"

Alfie was stunned. *She's got some nerve talking to me like that. Why, she doesn't even know me! Rose would never have been so bold.*

"Well, Missus," he paused peering at the tombstone, "Missus Murdoch. I really don't think it's any of your business how my Rose and I got on." He glanced at the marker again to make out the name. "Was your husband, Angus, such a model of virtue?"

"Hmph!" she sniffed. "Angus wasn't no model of nothin'. He was a dried up old fart! Just sat around like a turd on the grass. Never wanted to go anywhere or do nothin.' I can still see him parked in his chair in his underwear and socks readin' his newspaper. We didn't have a lot in common, either. He had the soul of a bachelor and he shoulda' stayed that way." She unravelled her story a little further.

She said she got on his nerves. Angus would play little games with her by not coming into a room where she was so he wouldn't have to listen to her or talk to her. Sometimes when she came down the stairs, she'd see the curtain on the kitchen door swaying and she knew he'd been there but had hurried out when he heard her footsteps. But she was wise to him and she would call out to him or find him lurking in another room behind a closed door. She would talk to him, but he only heard her voice not her words. He'd nod and grunt behind his newspaper and hope she'd go away and leave him alone in blessed isolation. His desire for privacy and solitude became an obsession with him and a frustration for his sociable wife.

As he listened, Alfie felt some of his guilt fading. Maybe he hadn't been such a bad husband after all. At least he'd tried to interest Rose in something outside of the house. Many times he'd suggested a little trip or a movie but she wasn't interested in anything like that. He gave up after a few years. She seemed content with everything as it was. But Alfie became restless with the sameness and the boredom in his life.

When he was in his mid-forties, he felt his sexual energy drifting away. He blamed Rose's continual rejections. She didn't care much for a lot of sweaty bedroom activity and Alfie began to visit a brothel on the edge of town. In the beginning, he had felt guilty about it, but he reasoned, he was just a red-blooded male who had to take care of his needs any way he could. In the end, old age had robbed him of his virility and he remained in his sexless marriage with Rose. Now here he was at her grave, brazenly staring at the attractive woman standing before him.

"If you feel that way about your husband, why do you bother to visit his grave?" he asked.

"Well, you could say I jest want to make sure he's still down there!" She laughed a deep throaty laugh.

Although he couldn't say why, Alfie was drawn to this woman. He usually went for the shy, timid type where he could exert his authority. But this woman's frankness intrigued him.

"Name's Mary." She stuck out her hand. "But just call me Queenie. Everybody calls me Queenie."

"Uh, Alfie Long," he stammered. "Pleased to make your acquaintance, uh, Queenie." They shook hands.

"How are ya gettin' along without yer wife?" Queenie asked, nodding toward Rose's grave. Her brown eyes were locked onto his. "I'll bet you don't even know how to boil water!" she teased. "Or worse, where to find the kettle!" Her laughter split the silence of the graveyard.

Alfie smiled in spite of himself. Rose had always kept the kettle on the boil for tea. But Queenie was right. He'd made a right mess of things since Rose died. He couldn't find anything and when he did find it, he didn't know what to do with it. He blamed Rose for never wanting him in her kitchen. She said he was just a nuisance.

"Tell ya what," Queenie said. "You look to me like you could use a good meal. Why don't ya come home with me fer supper. I've got a lovely pot of chicken stew on the stove, and I'll toss in a few dumplins' to spruce it up. And just this mornin' I made hot biscuits and an apple pie. How does that sound to you, Mr. Alfie Long?"

Alfie's taste buds were tingling. He hadn't had a good dinner in weeks. His friends didn't bother to invite him over any more, and he'd never invite himself. He didn't want anyone feeling sorry for him.

He pondered Queenie's offer. What would his friends think of him cavorting around with a strange woman? Well, Rose was gone now and the invitation to dinner was beginning to outweigh what anyone might think of him.

"Well, take your time, old man," Queenie chortled as she waited for an answer. "Don't do me no favours!"

"OK! OK! You talked me into it, but you'll have to show me the way. That's my car parked over there." Alfie pointed to his gray Chrysler parked outside the gate. "Where's your car?"

"Oh, I don't have a car," Queenie said. "I walked here."

"Well then. I'll drive and you direct," he said as Queenie spun around and headed for the gate ahead of him.

As Alfie drove, he thought of Rose and how quiet she was whenever she sat in the car beside him. He couldn't believe that he, Alfie Long, was driving some strange woman home to have dinner with her. And that he was actually enjoying her chatter!

He sat in Queenie's kitchen watching as she mixed up the dumplings and dropped the little balls of dough into the simmering pot of stew. He looked around the room. Spotless! Ship-shape! A tidy cook. Not like Rose. Other comparisons spun unbidden to his mind. Queenie looked about fifty-five. Rose had been much older. The two women didn't resemble each other in any way. Rose had been a tall, large-boned woman with a melancholy face. Queenie was a small woman, plump but not fat, with a face inviting friendship. Her silvery-white hair touched her shoulders in soft waves. Alfie liked it much better than the gray bun Rose had worn at the nape of her neck.

Queenie felt him staring at her and when she looked at him her large brown eyes seemed to penetrate his very thoughts.

She set a plate of hot biscuits before him and a jar of homemade apple jelly. She sat down opposite him at the kitchen table and poured the tea.

"Now don't go fillin' yerself up with them biscuits and jelly," she admonished as Alfie reached out. "I'll be dishin' up supper in a few minutes, or just as soon as I get these friggin' dumplins' cooked." Alfie was taken aback by her bossiness. And even more surprising, he enjoyed the attention. Her simple ways amused him.

The hours drifted by. As Queenie and Alfie ate dinner and talked, they became better acquainted. They talked about Rose and Angus and their past lives.

"You know Alfie, me and Angus never talked like this," Queenie said.

Alfie nodded, stuffing a dumpling into his mouth. "I know what you mean. Rose and I didn't either. We didn't have much in common. Why'd you stay with Angus, then, if you were unhappy?"

"Where would I go, Alfie? Where? It's different fer a woman. Back in them days it was a disgrace to walk out on yer husband. You'd be branded as a Jezebel. You stayed and put up with whatever was there. Whenever I complained, my father would say, 'You made your bed, girl, now lie in it.' Well, I got fed up with bein' ignored all the time, except of course when HE needed somethin'. I got even with him though."

"And how did you do that?" Alfie asked.

"Well, I moved out of our bedroom and refused to have anythin' to do with him." She pressed her lips together in satisfaction.

"I'll bet he didn't like that!" Alfie scoffed. He thought of the many times he'd forced himself on Rose. She'd just lie there stiff as a corpse. He wondered if she'd stayed with him because, like Queenie, she had nowhere else to go.

"I'm sure he never missed me for a second!" Queenie answered as she clattered the dirty dishes into the sink. "I'm gonna leave these for later," she said and she steered Alfie into the parlour.

"Make yerself comfy," she said plumping up the pillows on the sofa.

Alfie sat down. Queenie kicked off her shoes and sat beside him, tucking her feet under her.

"You never did tell me how Angus died. Was it a heart attack, Queenie?"

"He died of a stroke and believe me, it sure weren't from excitement." Queenie giggled covering her mouth.

"What kind of work did ya do, Alfie?" she asked, changing the subject.

"Oh, I used to build houses. I designed them and built them. I built a nice house for Rose and me. She seemed very fond of it." Did she really like it, he wondered? He was beginning to feel that he never really knew his wife or what she actually thought about anything.

For the next two or three months Alfie saw Queenie regularly. In the beginning his only reason for getting together with her was for a home-cooked meal, but as time went on, he found he enjoyed her company too. She was so full of life and her down-to-earth humour was refreshing. Sometimes he would drive over to the graveyard hoping he'd see her there.

"Wanna' go on a picnic tomorrow?" Queenie asked as they sat together in her kitchen one evening after supper. "I'll bring the grub and wine. You drive."

"Where did you have in mind?" Alfie always liked to know the plan in advance.

"You'll see when we git there. It'll be a surprise! Bet you never had a picnic there before!" she teased.

Alfie couldn't recall ever having been on a picnic with Rose. She wouldn't have wanted to go anyway.

The next day, he picked up Queenie at noon. She was loaded down with bags of food, a couple of bottles of wine, a card table and two folding chairs. Alfie put it all in the trunk of his car.

"Where to, Queen?" he asked with a new feeling of light-heartedness as he slid behind the wheel.

"To the cemetery, Alfie. We're gonna have a picnic with Angus and Rose and all the other dearly departed there."

She grinned at the horrified look on his face.

"We can't have a picnic there!" Alfie exploded. "What will people think? They'll think we're both crazy, that's what!"

"I don't give a tinker's damn what anybody thinks," Queenie laughed. "And neither should you! Live yer own life, Alfie. Enjoy the freedom now that you've got it. There ain't nothin' like it!"

Alfie was quiet as he drove to the cemetery. He'd never felt he'd had the freedom to do anything. Rose wouldn't have stopped him. But she'd have that wounded look in her eyes. He couldn't deal with that. She'd often made him feel like he was caught in a net.

He pulled up to the cemetery gate. Queenie carried the bags of food and wine. Alfie brought out the table and chairs.

"Here, Alfie. Right between Rose and Angus. It'll be their first picnic too." She pointed to a grassy spot between the two headstones.

Alfie set up the card table and the two folding chairs while Queenie rummaged in the bags for a tablecloth and napkins. Soon she had the table covered with plates of sandwiches, a jar of pickles, celery and carrot sticks, and two bottles of red wine. A chocolate cake nestled on a plate for dessert. They sat across from each other, surrounded by markers and memories. Queenie passed the sandwiches.

"Help yerself to the wine, Alfie," she said. "And pour some fer me." She held out her glass.

Alfie filled their glasses. Queenie lifted hers. "Here's to Rose and Angus. May they enjoy the picnic and rest in peace." She smiled, her brown eyes twinkling.

Alfie touched his glass to hers. He looked around hoping there was no one in the cemetery to see them.

"Rose would never believe this!" he said suddenly. "A picnic in the graveyard!"

"Din't ya never do nothin' fun or crazy, Alfie?"

"Nope! Rose wouldn't have done it even if I'd asked her. She was a real homebody." What would she have liked to do, he wondered.

"Well, I used to go off sometimes but never with Angus." Queenie said. "He wasn't much for the outdoors. Except for his garden. He'd sit out there for hours doin' nothin'. Just watchin' the grass grow!"

They finished eating and sat back to enjoy the sunny day. They were silent, deep in memories. Queenie closed her eyes. She held her smooth face up to the sun's rays. Alfie felt at peace.

The bells of St. Basil's Church sounded the Angelus. Barn swallows, startled from their nests in the belfry, twittered overhead. A pair of velvet-winged butterflies settled on Rose's tombstone. Then in a flash of black and yellow they flew away. Alfie watched, envious of their freedom as they floated up on a column of air into the open sky. Suddenly he felt an overwhelming sense of release descend upon him. He looked over at Queenie. She opened her eyes and smiled at him as though she'd read his thoughts.

"Do you think we should get married or something, Queenie?" he asked.

Under the Rose

They might have gone on that way forever had one of them not up and died. For fifteen years they'd spent their summers at the little island cottage on the Manitou River behind Tamarack's lumber mill until the day Judith Barnes died.

They'd lived together for forty years in an apartment in Toronto. Judith had been a choreographer for a ballet company, and Anna Moran had been her accompanist. The cottage on the river was their refuge. They'd bought it together the year before they retired in 1938 to get away from the heat and clamour of the city. They'd spent most of their summers there when they weren't off travelling in Europe or visiting friends in the States. In Tamarack, they'd joined the United Church and had registered in the church roster as Judith Barnes and Anna Moran, sisters. Judith had never married. Anna, on the other hand, had mentioned a deceased husband to some of the village women. When they'd asked about him, Anna just waved her hand and said, "Oh well, my dears, it was so long ago." So they stopped asking and he was soon forgotten.

Judith and Anna became an active part of the village life. Their worldly travels had greatly impressed the local women, most of whom had never been further than the next town. The two were undeniably different from the Tamarack women and were considered to be a bit eccentric. But both were liked all the same.

They'd organized a bridge club and taught the women how to play. They became involved in most of the church's fundraising events whenever they came up from the city. Sometimes they would travel to Toronto by train to see a play, go to the opera or visit friends and do some shopping. They'd stay down in the city for a week or so. Then one day, out of the blue, they'd be seen back in the village buying supplies for their cottage.

Judith, the older of the two, was a tall, gaunt woman of seventy with gray hair coiled in a braid at the back of her neck. She had a sharp face, and a long pointed nose. Her dark, wary eyes slithered in their sockets taking in everything and everybody. Her wide mouth embraced a set of large false teeth. She dressed in a tweedy English style. Black oxfords were the only shoes she wore, her feet hobbled by years of balancing 'en pointe'. She had a pinched, sullen look that defied her open and kind heart.

Anna was younger by ten years. She was short, just five feet, and overweight. She wore her straight black hair, (some thought dyed) in a short bob. Her blue eyes had that surprised look as though she'd just been told she'd won something. She dressed herself in wildly coloured ankle-length dresses and skirts. Ropes of chunky jewellery hung over her heavy bosom. A gold bracelet in the shape of a snake, its emerald eyes glittering, squeezed the flabby skin of her upper arm. She didn't wear a corset and her body quivered as she waddled around the cottage barefoot. Anna loved to talk and would prattle on about her life often letting her words get away from her. Judith would watch and listen silently, sometimes interrupting when she thought Anna's babbling was getting too personal. Judith was a more private person and felt she had to keep Anna in check. They were as different as two snowflakes, but they seemed to complement each other. They often entertained friends from the village at their little cottage, but no one had ever visited them in Toronto.

The day Judith died, Anna had gone up to the village to play bridge. Judith had begged off. She said she was too tired to listen to the chattering of the women and she already had a headache. She said she wouldn't be able to concentrate on the game.

"I'll do a little weeding in the garden," she said. "And perhaps I'll have a lie-down. You go on and enjoy yourself. I'll fix something later for our dinner."

"If you're not well, I'll stay with you. I don't mind." Anna moved toward the telephone.

"I wouldn't hear of it, dear. I'll be fine. Please don't worry about me."

Anna hesitated for a moment but decided that Judith knew best. After all, Judith always made the rules and Anna usually followed her decisions.

The ladies at the bridge club were concerned about Judith, clacking their busy tongues and shaking their heads in sympathy.

"She's looked a little peaked lately, I thought," Mrs. Wardell said.

"Yes, that's true," Anna agreed. "She's been doing a bit of fixing up around the cottage, painting her bedroom and making new drapes and a bedspread. I suppose she's been overdoing it a little. I'll have to get after her about that," she added. But she knew she'd never say anything. Judith would tell her to stop fussing.

"I hope she'll be able to help in the church bazaar next week," Mrs. Watts said. "She's planning to put up that beautiful lace tablecloth she's been working on. You know the one with the pineapple design. She brought it out and showed it to us at our last meeting at the cottage."

"I'm sure she'll be fine by then," Anna said as she shuffled the cards and finished dealing. The four women fell silent in concentration. A few hands were played as they chatted among themselves.

Later on, Mrs. Graham brought out refreshments. From a silver cake stand she sliced a towering banana cake piled high with whipped cream and edged with sliced bananas. She passed around wedges of it on small dessert plates with little silver cake forks wrapped in white linen napkins. Mrs. Watts filled bone china cups from the silver tea service that Mrs. Graham had spent the morning polishing. The women nibbled their cake, sipped their tea and discussed the up-coming church bazaar. At four o'clock everyone left for home. Anna walked alone over the little footbridge toward the cottage.

All was quiet as she opened the front door "I'm back, Judith!" she called. When there was no response she walked to the back of the cottage and went out into the garden. Judith was sitting in one of the deck chairs.

"I'm home, dear," Anna called out again walking toward her. "Are you feeling any better?"

Judith sat erect, her head to one side. Her soiled garden gloves lay on her lap.

"Asleep," muttered Anna as she reached out and took her hand. It felt icy cold and limp. She looked at Judith's eyes. They were wide-open, fixed and glassy. She fumbled for a pulse. She couldn't find one. She dropped the lifeless hand. A burst of cold sweat broke out under her arms. Tiny rivulets trickled between her breasts.

"Oh, my God!" she gasped. She turned and ran into the house. Her heart was drumming wildly. With shaking fingers, she dialed Dr. Mills.

"It's Anna Moran, Doctor. There's something wrong with Judith. She's not breathing and she's so cold. Please come! I don't know what to do!" She replaced the receiver softly as though not to disturb the dreadful quiet of the room.

Tears streamed down her cheeks. She was too weak to stand up. She rocked back and forth in her chair, moaning, mouth open, her breath shuddering. Her eyes were drawn to the window. She stood up and stumbled toward it. She stared out at Judith sitting upright in the garden chair. Her sudden appearance at the window disturbed a flock of birds pecking in the garden.

There was a knock at the door. She turned to answer it. It was Dr. Mills. He stepped inside and took Anna's hands in his.

"My dear Anna!" he said. He looked at her with compassion. Then quietly asked, "Where is she?" Anna led him out to the garden. As soon as Dr. Mills looked at Judith he knew the worst. "I'll call an ambulance," he said. "Come inside and sit down, Anna. There's nothing we can do for her now. I'm so sorry!" Anna buried her face in her hands.

Before long, two attendants arrived with a stretcher and Judith's body was carried across the little bridge to a waiting ambulance. Anna couldn't bear to watch. She stayed inside the cottage. When Dr. Mills had left, Anna sat alone in the deadly quiet. Outside, dusk was slowly shrouding the day.

"I shouldn't have left her," she whimpered to herself. "For once I should have listened to my own feelings. I shouldn't have let her change my mind." She sat for a long time thinking about her life and how she would manage without Judith.

She knew she had to make the phone call. It would be an ordeal, she knew that. She found the number in Judith's book, picked up the phone and dialed. A man's voice answered. "Gerald Thoms here."

"Hello, Gerald. It's Anna Moran." There was no response. Anna continued. "I'm afraid I have some bad news." There was a pause while Gerald waited for her to continue.

"This is very difficult." Anna's voice trembled and she waited a moment before she spoke again.

"It's your Aunt Judith, Gerald. I'm sorry to tell you that she passed away this afternoon." That was all she was able to say. She was afraid she would break down and begin crying again.

"Well, I'm sorry to hear that. I suppose I'll have to come up there and bring her body back to Toronto." Anna didn't answer. She hadn't even thought about that. Of course Gerald would get right to the point.

"Well, we never were close," Gerald continued. "Mother never saw eye to eye with either of you. What did she die of anyway?" Anna was shocked at his callous attitude.

"It was her heart, a massive coronary, the doctor said. She went very quickly."

"Well, that much is a blessing I suppose," he said. "I'll be up on the next train. I'll phone you with the time. Can you meet me? I don't know where you live."

"I'll be at the station," Anna assured him. "Will Beverly be coming with you?" Beverly was Gerald's wife. Anna had seen her only a few times since she and Gerald married ten years ago. They'd had three children whom she'd never met.

"Probably not. I'll let you know." The phone went dead.

~~

Gerald Thoms sat on the flowered chintz sofa in the cottage sitting room. Anna watched him as he fidgeted with his cigarette lighter. He was pretty much of a stranger to her. A stranger who'd never bothered with either Judith or herself in the forty years the two women had lived together. He must be close to fifty by now, she thought. She studied his balding head as he bent over the flame of the lighter. He was a tall thin man dressed in a stylish gray pin-striped suit.

Gerald stopped clicking the lighter and put it away in his jacket pocket. He lifted his head and stared at Anna with pale, cold eyes.

"I've arranged for an undertaker to meet me in Toronto," he said. "He'll take the body to the funeral home where I've made arrangements for her burial."

Anna stared at him. He'd done everything. It was all so quick as though he wanted to be rid of both of them as soon as possible. After a few minutes of silence, Gerald spoke again.

"I've checked through her personal papers with her lawyer in Toronto." Anna's eyes widened. Judith had never told her she'd had a lawyer. She opened her mouth to speak but Gerald went on. "And I'm sure you know, there's no will. I'm her sole beneficiary."

Anna and Judith had never thought they needed a will. Everything in the cottage and in their Toronto apartment was owned by both, equally. When they'd bought something, it was for both to enjoy. She vaguely remembered Judith suggesting getting a lawyer when they'd bought the cottage. But Anna didn't care about any of that and said so. She'd told Judith to do whatever she felt necessary. And that was the last she'd heard of it. She must have paid for all that by herself Anna thought, and she silently berated herself for not taking more of an interest in their affairs.

Gerald stood up. "Take anything you like from the cottage," he snapped. "I'll be selling the place as soon as I can. Everything here will be sold or auctioned off, but you can stay on until I find a buyer, if you wish."

Anna sat stunned. She stared at his impassive face. It was as if he was auctioning off her life. It would be all over in one stroke of a pen! She knew Judith would never have wanted this.

"When you get back to Toronto, Beverly and I'll come over to the apartment to see if there's anything she wants. I'll be lucky to unload all of this." He gestured around at the modest furnishings. Judith and Anna never wanted anything fancy in their cottage. It was just a place to relax away from the bustle of the city and they'd made it comfortable without spending a lot of money. Most of the furniture was from second-hand stores. The curtains, quilts, and tablecloths they'd made themselves.

He fancies he's being very generous, Anna thought. Doesn't he care I've lost everything? My companion of over forty years and now our little cottage? This stranger, who's never bothered with us, and now he's here to get every penny he can from our possessions? Anger began to spread into her grief. Anger at Gerald and his high-handed way of dumping her. She got up from her chair.

"No thank you, Gerald," she spoke softly. "I'll not stay on. Nor will I take anything from the cottage. You can have it all." Her voice quavered. Her eyes were drawn to Judith's tablecloth lying in her sewing basket. It would never see the raffle table now. She walked slowly into her bedroom, shut the door and took down a suitcase from on top of the wardrobe. Now that she was alone, she let the tears come. She desperately tried to stifle her sobs. Gerald was the last person on earth she wanted to hear her anguish.

She packed only the few clothes and jewellery that she'd kept at the cottage. In less than an hour she was back in the sitting room, dressed and ready to leave. She stood in the doorway holding her suitcase. Gerald was at the window looking out into the garden.

"Now let me see if I've got this straight," she said in a flat voice. "Everything here will be sold?"

Gerald turned and nodded.

"But I'll stay in our apartment in Toronto. And you and Beverly will come and remove anything you want. Is that correct?"

"That's right. But you don't have to leave right away. I said you could stay until the place is sold."

"That's so kind of you, Gerald." Anna spat out the words. "But I would rather go now." She picked up her bag and turned toward the door. Suddenly her eyes fell on Judith's tablecloth in the basket. She bent down, snatched it up and flung it over her shoulder. She flashed a look at Gerald that said, "You'll not have this!" Then she jerked open the door and marched out of the cottage for the last time, the tablecloth sweeping the ground behind her. She didn't look back.

Anna boarded the train and found a seat. She slammed down her suitcase and sat in the adjoining seat. She was exhausted and furious with Gerald's arrogance. She pounded her clenched fist on the window-sill. "The man is completely without scruples," she fumed. She took little sips of air through clenched teeth. Grief slowly softened her anger. She thought of Judith and her eyes filled with tears again. Why? she wailed silently. I loved her so much. Adored her. She was so precious to me and she loved me. I know she did!

The train jerked forward and pulled out of the station. As Anna stared out of the window, memories of their life together swamped her. The winter Judith had been sick with pneumonia. One night as they lay in bed, Judith had called softly to her, "Anna, Anna, come closer." Anna awoke and moved next to her.

"Don't ever leave me, please! Stay with me forever," Judith pleaded. Anna held her, whispering, "You don't have to worry when I'm here. You know that." She'd put her hand on Judith's burning cheek and brushed back her hair.

"You're so good to me," Judith sighed. They drifted off to sleep wrapped in each other's arms.

The next morning she'd bathed Judith and helped her into a clean nightgown.

She'd combed and braided her hair and brought her breakfast. While Judith ate, Anna had read to her.

"Oh God," Anna whispered, "how can I let her go!" The train clattered onward.

~~

At the Tamarack Realty Office, Robert Chambers sat behind his desk shuffling papers. Gerald sat across from him, his fingers tapping the arm of the chair.

"Now, Mr. Thoms," Chambers said glancing up at Gerald, "there's something about your claim that puzzles me. You say you're Miss Barnes's only living relative. But I believe that her sister, Mrs. Moran, is the rightful heir to the cottage and its contents. It was jointly owned by the two women, wasn't it?"

"No, it wasn't! I'm the rightful heir!" Gerald shot back.

"Do you have any papers to prove that you're the beneficiary?"

"There are no papers," Gerald barked. "It was just cash and a handshake with the farmer who owned it originally. A lawyer in Toronto has the deed and there's only one name on it. Aunt Judith's. Anna Moran's name isn't anywhere on the document."

"Seems a bit strange to me," drawled Chambers. "I've known those girls for years. Perhaps I'd better give that lawyer a call."

"Oh! that's just great! Are you calling me a liar?" Gerald snapped.

"No," drawled Chambers, "it just seems odd since those sisters were so close. I think it's best to check out the facts."

Gerald jumped to his feet and began to pace back and forth across the room. Suddenly he stopped and leaned across the desk, his hands gripping the edge.

"Look," he said through gritted teeth. "What I'm trying to tell you is that Anna and Judith weren't SISTERS! They weren't related at all!"

"What do you mean not sisters?" Chambers challenged.

Gerald shoved his flushed face closer, inches from Chambers.

"I mean Aunt Judith and Anna Moran were LOVERS!" he shouted. "FILTHY LOVERS!"

Chambers sat stunned as Gerald's words echoed off the walls and faded through the open window, floating across the village like spores, taking root, growing and spreading from the lips of the Tamarack women.

The Wheel of Life
The Flight

After the ceremony the guests left for the reception at the bride's family farm. Some walked the distance of two miles, others came in horse-drawn carts. Long tables draped with crocheted tablecloths had been set up in the yard. Women bustled about laying out large platters of chicken, kielbasa rings, heaping bowls of golabki, pierogi and steaming tureens of barszcz. Dishes of ogorek and sour cream were added. Mountains of chleb teetered on plates. Vodka and whiskey bottles were placed at intervals on the tables. Off to one side, a large table groaned under the weight of tortes, paczek and ciastko, all hidden under a white sheet. Children shrieked and chased each other around the yard, pausing only to peek under the sheet and snatch a treat. Unlike the adults, they were unaware of the tensions between their homeland, Poland, and neighbouring Russia.

Friends and relatives put aside their fears today and gathered at the farmhouse to celebrate the wedding of Ursula Machatsky and Tomasz Krasinski.

A wooden platform had been erected for dancing, and the late-comers were greeted with the sounds of accordion music. Couples whirled to the lively polka tunes. Their colourful costumes blurred the air as shawl tassels flapped and white linen petticoats peeked out from under billowing skirts.

Ursula and Tomasz watched the festivities from the head table that had been decorated with white and silver paper hearts. Their families and wedding attendants sat beside them, tapping their feet to the rhythm. Bunches of wild flowers tied with colourful ribbons decorated the verandah posts.

The bride and groom were very young. Ursula was a vivacious eighteen-year-old and Tomasz had just reached his twenty-first birthday. Her laughing round face and blonde braided coronet were a contrast to her husband's dark hair and his solemn expression. They wore the colourful, embroidered wedding costumes in the traditional style.

The young couple had grown up on neighbouring farms by the village of Dabrowa near the border between Russia and Poland. They'd attended the rural school together until they were forced to leave to help out on their family's farms. They often met at weddings and festive occasions in the parish hall, and they had fallen in love.

After Father Klemkowski had blessed the bride and groom and given thanks for the abundance of food, the guests sat down to the feast provided by the neighbouring women. Gossip was bandied about and loud laughter rang out as stories and crude jokes circulated. Friendly teasing brought a blush to Ursula's cheeks. The drinking was hearty and folk songs erupted as men pounded their glasses on the table keeping time to the music. It seemed nothing could spoil the young couple's happiness. But fate with some unexpected and unwanted human help had other plans for Tomasz and Ursula.

There was so much shouting and singing that no one heard the sharp clatter of galloping horses, the crack of gunfire and the roaring voices thundering through the gate and into the yard. A dozen wild-eyed horses reared up, foaming at the mouth, sweat glistening. The wedding party jumped up from the tables and ran toward the woods as Russian soldiers took aim and fired into the crowd of merrymakers.

Tomasz grabbed Ursula and the decorated basket of money from the table. While the horsemen were chasing and shooting at the fleeing guests, Tomasz and Ursula quietly slipped away. They raced into the hayfield and hid in a haystack, clinging together. The sounds of gunfire and the screams from the dying echoed throughout the long night. In the morning, a deathly silence hung over everything. Fires from the torched village had reddened the sky.

Ursula and Tomasz crept out from their hiding place, cold and hungry. They brushed bits of hay from their clothes and looked around. They saw no signs of life.

"We have to go back to the farm, Tomasz!" Ursula cried. "We have to know what's happened to our parents! To our friends!"

Tomasz put his arms around her. "No, Ursula, it's

too dangerous. If the soldiers see us they'll kill us! We have to get away from here!" They crept across the empty field and into the woods. They had no idea where they were going. To stay would mean certain death or a train to Siberia, and Tomasz knew if that happened he would never see Ursula again.

They traveled slowly along dusty roads and through open fields, eating whatever they could buy or beg. They bedded down in barns and haystacks and in the forests to avoid suspicion. Tomasz broke branches from the trees and they slept on beds of pine boughs. The nights were warm and windless as they lay in each other's arms under a star-studded sky.

"We'll go north to Danzig," Tomasz said. "We'll be safe there."

After three weeks of walking, Ursula sat down by the roadside. She was crying from the searing pain of her blistered, swollen feet. Tomasz knelt down beside her and gathered her in his arms. He carried her on his back the last few miles into Danzig, stopping at intervals to rest.

The sights and sounds of the city overwhelmed the young couple. Danzig was the first city they'd ever seen. They'd never been away from their parents' farms except for short trips into Dabrowa. Exhausted, they rested on a bench in the village square. Tomasz tried to form a plan. He looked at Ursula. Her eyes were closed and her pale face was pinched in pain. What was he going to do? There was no turning back. He touched her shoulder. Her thin body was slumped against the bench.

"Stay here Ursula, he said. "I'll come back for you. I'll go down to the docks and if I can find work for us on a ship, we'll leave Poland and start a new life away from here."

Ursula opened her eyes. "Don't leave me here, Tomasz! I'm frightened!" she begged.

"Don't worry, kochany! I'll be back very soon." He kissed her, stroking her hair. Then he stood up and walked away. Ursula looked after him with panic in her eyes.

Time dragged by slowly. Ursula didn't dare move from the bench. She saw two Russian soldiers walking toward her. Tiny needles of fear shot through her. She pulled her shawl tightly around her and tucked some of the bulky wedding dress behind her. She lowered her eyes. The two men stopped and stared at her for a moment, and then moved on. They looked back laughing and joking in Russian. Other people passed by but Ursula saw none of them and they took no notice of her. She was very frightened. The afternoon was fading into dusk.

"What if he can't find me!" she moaned softly. Her hands twisted the corner of the shawl, tighter and tighter. She was beginning to panic. Finally she saw Tomasz coming toward her. He sat down beside her and took her hands in his. She gripped his strong fingers as if she would never let go.

"I've found a ship going to Canada, Ursula. The captain has agreed to hire us. You will cook and I'll scrub decks, clean cabins and anything else to earn our passage. The ship sails tonight. We'll work our way across the ocean."

Ursula began to protest. "Tomasz! Where are we going? I'm scared!"

"Don't be afraid, kochany. It'll be good." He hugged her shivering body close to him. He told her how he'd found the ship. "It's a Polish ship called The Bathory," he said. "It's carrying coal to Halifax. To Canada, Ursula! We'll start a new life in a new country!" His eyes shone with excitement. She wished she could feel as confident. She gave him a fleeting smile, and prayed that he was right.

"Ursula," he murmured, "I want you to stay here just a little longer while I go and get some ointment for your feet. I'll get something for us to eat too." Tomasz patted her arm. "I won't be long," he assured her.

When he returned they sat together on the bench and ate a little of the food he had brought. Tomasz rubbed some of the soothing salve on Ursula's swollen feet.

On their way to the ship they stopped in a clothing store. They had to replace their badly soiled and torn wedding garments with something suitable for working on board the ship. They bought two pairs of trousers and three shirts for Tomasz and two skirts and blouses for Ursula. They added some new undergarments and two warm jackets to the pile on the counter. Tomasz counted out the money. He grimaced when he saw how little of it was left.

The captain of The Bathory greeted them as they came on board. He directed a deckhand to take them to their tiny cabin. They fell into their bunks and were soon fast asleep as the ship sailed out of Danzig at sunset.

The Journey

Ursula and Tomasz had never been on a ship. They didn't know that a rough crossing could mean seasickness. But the weather was with them, long sunny days on a mercifully smooth ocean and cool evenings when they tumbled into bed exhausted.

Tomasz worked hard at his chores, and Ursula spent most of her time in the ship's galley. She was a great cook and the crew enjoyed her hearty Polish fare. Even the captain, a taciturn man, would often come into the galley to thank her and sample some of her preparations for their evening meal.

Some nights the young couple would join the sailors on deck and they sang and danced to accordion music. But usually they kept to themselves in the evenings, washing their few clothes and spreading them around the little cabin to dry. They rested whenever they could. The long trek from the farm and the emotional stress of leaving their families had drained their energies.

One morning, after nearly a month at sea, Tomasz had just finished scrubbing the deck. As he tossed the bucket of water over the side, he looked up and saw Halifax harbour in the distance. He ran to the galley where Ursula was preparing the midday meal.

"Ursula! Ursula!" he shouted. "Come quick! I can see a city ahead! We'll be docking soon." Ursula stood beside him at the ship's railing straining to see.

"See, there's the harbour!" Tomasz pointed as the city of Halifax loomed ahead.

"Oh, Tomasz! It's so beautiful!" Ursula's excitement mounted. Her fears for their future were beginning to lessen.

They'd made the decision while on board the ship to go to Stanley Kowalski's farm which was located near the little village of Tamarack in Ontario. Tomasz and Stanley had grown up together on neighbouring farms in Poland. When Stanley left five years ago he'd wanted Tomasz to come with him, but Tomasz didn't want to leave Ursula whom he was planning to marry some day. Stanley told him that if ever he changed his mind, to let him know and he would help him get started in Canada. He wrote to Tomasz often about his farm and how happy he was, always encouraging him to join him.

Before they left the ship the captain exchanged what remained of their Polish money into Canadian dollars and added more, paying them for their hard work. He drew a small map for them showing the route to the Halifax train station. Since neither Ursula nor Tomasz could speak any English, he wrote a note to the ticket agent requesting two tickets to the village of Tamarack. As they stood at the ship's gangplank preparing to go ashore, Tomasz shook the captain's hand. "Thank you very much for your kindness, Sir," he said. "You've given us a chance for a new life. My wife and I are very grateful."

"Good luck to you, Tomasz. I'm sure you'll both do well!"

At the railroad station, Tomasz handed the note and some money to the ticket agent who read it and placed two tickets to Tamarack on the counter. In the late afternoon, they boarded the train with their few belongings and a basket of food they were able to put together after much pointing and nodding to the clerk in the grocery store.

"We'll have to learn English, Ursula, and the sooner the better or we'll never get on in this country," Tomasz said as they left the shop.

On the train Ursula sat close to Tomasz and together they watched the landscape change from the forests of Nova Scotia to the rolling hills of Quebec. Tomasz shook his head in amazement when he saw the thriving farms along the St.

Lawrence River. Everything looked so peaceful. He watched silently as the long, narrow fields flew by. Never in his wildest dreams did he believe a country could be so big.

"This country will be good for us, Ursula," he murmured. But she was fast asleep, her head resting on his shoulder.

Each day the train carried them further toward Tamarack. Whenever they could, they got off to stretch their legs and to buy a little food. As they crossed the border into Ontario, Tomasz noticed the changing landscape. The land was rocky and the farms were smaller and not as prosperous-looking as those in Quebec. He closed his eyes and smiled when he thought of how surprised Stanley would be to see them.

Three nights and four days later, with a final jolt and a sudden stop, the train arrived at Tamarack. On the station platform Tomasz approached a short, thick-set fellow loading provisions on a wagon. He pulled one of Stanley's letters out of his pocket and pointed to the address. He held out some coins. The man nodded and waived the money aside. "Get in," he said. "I'll take you there." Tomasz stood mutely by the wagon. The driver pointed for them to get in the back. He finished loading and climbed up, snapping the reins on the horses' rumps. They started off down the dirt road.

"Where are you from?" the driver asked. Tomasz opened his hands in a helpless gesture. It was obvious that he didn't understand. They rode on in silence.

At Stanley's farm gate, the man reined in the horses. He pointed to a small house set back a short distance from the road. "Kowalski's," he said, nodding toward the farm.

"Dzieki! Dzieki!" Tomasz said, shaking hands with the driver. He jumped down from the wagon and held out his arms for Ursula. The driver handed them their baggage and drove off.

The Gift

Stanley Kowalski peered through a crack in the open door. It was turning dark and it was a few minutes before he recognized his visitors.

"Good God!" he shouted swinging open the door. "Where did you two come from? Come in, come in." He grabbed them in his arms, hugging them and pounding Tomasz on his back. Stanley was almost dancing with joy. "I can't believe it! You finally came! What took you so long, Tomasz?"

The exhausted young couple sat in the kitchen while Stanley laid the table with bread and cheese and sausage. While they ate, Stanley besieged them with questions

"How did you get here, Tomasz? What's happening back home? I haven't heard from my family in months. Are my parents OK? My brothers and sisters?" He fired questions at Tomasz.

"We don't know about your family," Ursula murmured as she began to tell him what happened at their wedding. The Russian soldiers, the shooting, the screaming, their own escape.

"Did anyone else escape?" asked Stanley, his face ashen. His hope for his family's safety was dwindling. "Maybe they were taken prisoners and are locked up somewhere in Russia. They wouldn't be allowed to write letters. Or maybe they're all dead," he whispered.

Ursula sat with her head in her hands, her thin body swaying on the chair.

"She's worn out, Tomasz!" Stanley said. "Come Ursula, Tomasz. I'll show you to the bedroom. You both need to rest." He picked up their bags and took them to a small bedroom at the back of the house. He brought some bed linen and pillows from a closet and helped Tomasz make up the bed. In the doorway he turned to Tomasz.

"If you're not too tired, Tomasz, come back and tell me more. I want to hear all of it."

Tomasz tucked Ursula into the soft feather bed and kissed her good night. She was already asleep. He tip-toed from the room and sat down with Stanley in the kitchen.

The two men talked long into the night. Stanley was angry. "Those Russian bastards can't leave us alone!" he shouted. Tomasz was nodding, his eyes closing. He couldn't fight off sleep any longer. It was nearly dawn when he bade Stanley good night and slipped into bed beside Ursula.

The next morning after breakfast, the two men walked around the farm. Tomasz helped Stanley with the chores. Ursula stayed behind working in the kitchen.

Stanley had never married. He was a shy man and his farm kept him too busy to think about looking for a wife.

Tomasz asked Stanley why he had picked this place to farm. "The soil is thin and so many rocks." He picked up a handful of earth, letting it slide through his fingers. "It'd be a short growing period. Why'd you stay here, Stanley?"

Stanley laughed. "This is as far as I could go with the money I had. I always intended to move farther west later on, but I got to like it here. The people are friendly and so I stayed. I grow enough corn and wheat to sell, and my vegetable garden keeps me fed all summer. Can't eat it all by myself so I give a lot of it away. There are plenty of poor families here, too, Tomasz. In the winter I cut ice from the bay and store it in sawdust in the shed. Everybody wants ice for their iceboxes in the summer. I live pretty good."

Tomasz nodded. "Maybe I'll stay around here for a while too. " he said. "It would be good to have you nearby." How could he make a living here? How could he provide for Ursula and himself with no money? Stanley sensed his dilemma.

"If you want to stay, Tomasz, you and Ursula can live here with me and help me on the farm. I'm going to need an extra hand. I'm planning to buy the land on the other side of this field and raise some cattle." He waved his arm toward the vacant field. "I can't do it all by myself. Talk it over with Ursula. If she says it's OK, then stay. I've plenty of room. She can look after the house while we take care of the farm. We'll share whatever profits there are. That way you can get your own place sooner."

They walked back to the house. Ursula had the noon meal waiting. Tomasz didn't say anything to her about Stanley's offer. He wanted to wait until they were alone. As they lay in bed that night, he told her what Stanley had suggested. Ursula was silent.

"What do you think, Ursula?" he asked. "Do you want to stay here with Stanley? It'll give us a chance to save some money for our own place."

"I think it would be good, Tomasz. We've no money to buy land now. If we stay on here we can help Stanley and put some money aside too." She paused, reflecting. "It's so kind of him. Yes," she agreed, " we should stay here and help him, Tomasz."

"Good, good! I'll tell him tomorrow. It's true. We haven't any money but with a place to live and a chance to earn some... well, someday." His voice trailed off. They fell asleep wrapped in each other's arms and dreaming of their future.

~~

For six years, Stanley and Tomasz worked the land together. The little farm flourished. Tomasz opened a bank account at the Tamarack Bank and each week he'd put aside whatever money he could spare. The account slowly grew and the young couple's dream of having their own place became closer to reality.

Toward the end of their sixth year together, Ursula noticed that Stanley seemed listless and at times he was unable to carry out the simplest task. Tomasz had taken over most of the heavy chores.

One night Ursula was awakened by noises from Stanley's bedroom. She could hear him moving around during the night. At breakfast the next morning he didn't eat anything. She was worried and mentioned her fears to Tomasz.

"There's something wrong with him, Tomasz. I think he should go to the doctor."

Tomasz agreed. " I know. He's looked kind of pale lately, and sometimes I've seen him holding his side as if he was in pain. Just yesterday I saw him leaning against one of the horse stalls. He was almost doubled over. I asked him if he was all right. But he just waved me off and said he was fine."

A few nights later, Ursula was awakened again by the sound of something falling. "Tomasz!" she whispered shaking his arm. "Wake up! I heard something. Listen! I can hear Stanley groaning!" Tomasz leaped out of bed and opened the bedroom door. Stanley lay on the floor, his legs drawn up tight against his stomach. He had vomited and was gasping for breath.

"Stanley, Stanley! What's wrong?" Tomasz cried as he knelt beside him.

"Terrible pain," he whispered, holding his side.

"You're going to the doctor, my friend!" Tomasz lifted him up and laid him on the bed. Ursula appeared in the doorway, her eyes anxious.

"What is it, Tomasz? What's happened?"

"I don't know but I'm taking him to Tamarack to Dr. Mills. Help me clean him up and get yourself dressed." Stanley was moaning. Tomasz turned to Ursula. "Get some blankets and make a bed for him in the wagon. Then come back and stay with him while I hitch up the horses."

Ursula pulled the comforter off the bed and gathered up some blankets from their bed. She threw on some clothes and ran outside placing the comforter in the bottom of the wagon and spreading the blankets on top. Then she hurried back to Stanley. Tomasz left to bring the horses from the barn. He backed them into the traces and fastened the harnesses. Back in the house, he gathered up Stanley in his arms and carried him to the wagon. He laid him on the makeshift bed and tucked the blankets around him. Ursula climbed in cradling Stanley's head in her lap. She wiped heavy beads of perspiration from his face. "It'll be all right, Stanley," she murmured. "Dr. Mills will know what to do. Try not to move. We'll be there soon." Tomasz touched the reins to the horses' rumps.

It was three miles to the village of Tamarack. Tomasz didn't want to drive the horses too fast over the rough gravel road for fear of causing Stanley more pain. In just under an hour he pulled the horses up beside Dr. Mills' house. He pounded on the door to awaken the doctor. They carried Stanley, gasping in pain, into the examination room. The doctor looked at Tomasz.

"It's his appendix," he said. "It's ruptured and it's very serious. I can't do anything for him here. I don't have the proper facilities. We'll have to take him to the hospital in the next town. Help me get him into my car."

Ursula sat in the back with Stanley. Tomasz climbed in the front. He looked at the doctor with questioning eyes.

"There's always a chance that the inflammation could clear up with proper treatment," Dr. Mills said. "So let's just pray for that."

Stanley had slipped into unconsciousness.

In the hospital emergency room a quick examination confirmed the doctor's diagnosis. Stanley was slowly being poisoned by a burst appendix. The hospital staff worked all night to save him as the poison spread through his body.

When the operation was over, Dr. Mills joined Tomasz and Ursula in the waiting room. He sat down beside them, still wearing his hospital garb.

"Stanley's in very bad shape, I'm sorry to say. He should have come to me before this." He looked with sympathy at their worried faces. "I have to tell you that he's a very sick man, but we'll do everything we can for him."

Tomasz tried to explain in his halting English why they hadn't brought him in sooner. "He never tell us he's sick, Doctor. We worry he don't look good. I ask many times if he's OK. I see him holding his belly. He say he's fine. He think he eat something no good. If I know I would make him come to you."

"Well, we'll do what we can. He's asleep now. You both go home. Come back tomorrow. Hopefully we'll see some improvement."

~~

Ursula was quiet on the trip back to the farm. Her lips moved in a silent prayer. Tomasz was deep in thought. What if Stanley doesn't survive? What will happen to his farm? What will happen to us?

They spent much of the night worrying about their friend. In the morning after they'd done the necessary chores, they hitched up the horses and returned to the hospital. Dr. Mills saw them waiting outside Stanley's room. He came quickly toward them. He put his hand on Tomasz's shoulder.

"Mr. Krasinski, I'm afraid the operation wasn't successful. We did everything humanly possible, but the poison had spread too far and too fast. Stanley died during the night. I'm very sorry."

Ursula put her hand to her mouth uttering a small cry. Tomasz stood in shock trying to gather his thoughts.

"He got no family here, Doctor. What can I do? I don't know the ways here."

Dr. Mills felt sorry for the young couple so filled with grief. "I'll help you with the funeral arrangements if you wish," he said. "I'll contact the parish priest. I believe he was Catholic, was he not?"

"Tak! tak!" Ursula spoke up. "I like for you to do very much!"

Most of the people in Tamarack knew Stanley and liked him because of his generosity with his garden. They joined Ursula and Tomasz at the simple funeral. Stanley was buried in the little graveyard in Tamarack.

~~

The following day, they looked through Stanley's papers that he'd kept in a shoe-box under his bed. There were bills owing and the funeral to be paid for. All of Stanley's business transactions were in English. Tomasz tried but he couldn't understand the legal language of the documents. He gathered up the papers and took them to Mr. Grant, the bank manager in Tamarack. They sorted through the pile on Mr. Grant's desk.

"Here's his last will and testament, Tomasz. I helped him draw it up a couple of years ago." A smile spread across his face as he handed it to Tomasz.

"Well, it's a nice surprise for you, Tomasz. Stanley has left his farm and all his possessions to you."

"Oh, no! Dat can't be!" Tomasz exclaimed. "He has family in old country. They get his farm, not me! No, no! Not for me his farm!"

"It's all very legal, Tomasz!" Mr. Grant assured him. "The farm is yours, all right. I asked him about his family when we drew up the will. He told me he hadn't heard from anyone in Poland for years. He told me about the massacre on your wedding day. He was so sure there was no one left of his family that he wanted you to have the farm if anything should happen to him. He said you'd worked hard to help him and it was what he wanted to do for you and your wife."

Mr. Grant held out his hand. "Congratulations, Tomasz," he said, his face beaming.

All the way back to the farm, Tomasz kept shaking his head. He couldn't believe it. His old friend had placed his farm and his life's work in his care.

Ursula was as dumbfounded as Tomasz when he gave her the news.

"Look how much he's given us, Tomasz! Everything we've dreamed of!"

She burst into tears. "Oh, Stanley! Stanley!" she sobbed. "Thank you!"

The Visitor

Tomasz Krasinski stood inside the screen door. It was late. A curtain of blackness had descended over the little farm. He could see the flickering light of the lantern that he'd hung on the gatepost at the bottom of the hill. He'd put it there to guide his grandson, Victor, who was bringing his bride from Toronto for a visit.

At night the darkness in the country was impenetrable. It was easy to miss your destination without something to guide you.

Ursula was bustling about in the kitchen. He could hear the clatter of dishes and the rattle of cutlery as she prepared a spread for the visitors.

"Ursula! Ursula!" he cried. "They're coming!"

The car stopped at the gate. He saw Victor get out, unhook the lantern and extinguish the flame. He got back in and the car moved slowly up the hill. Tomasz smiled. Victor had remembered about the lantern. When he was a boy living on the farm with them, he would watch for its glowing light when he and his grandfather came home at night after a day at market in Tamarack.

Ursula ran in from the kitchen, wiping her hands on her apron. She stood eagerly beside Tomasz.

Victor and his wife came in juggling luggage and boxes of gifts. Excited shouting in Polish rang out and a tumult of hugging and kissing followed. The old couple were barely able to contain their excitement. When the loud greetings died down, Victor introduced Renee.

"Babcia, Dziadek, this is Renee, my wife." There was an awkward moment of silence. Tomasz and Ursula were shy with outsiders, and were embarrassed about their poor English. They smiled timidly at Renee, grasped her smooth hands and held them in their knobby work-worn fingers.

"I'm so pleased to finally meet you!" Renee gushed.

"Velcome, velcome," Ursula cried. "Ve happy you comin, Dzieci."

When Ursula was nervous she would lapse into Polish in mid-sentence. It made Renee feel like an outsider. She didn't understand their language. Her background was French Canadian. The two couples stood rigid and tense. Ursula grabbed Victor's arm.

"Come to kitchen!" she shouted. "I make coffee. I bake nice tort for you."

Renee was relieved when Victor refused. "No, Babcia! We aren't hungry. We've eaten already. It's late and we're tired. It's late for you and Dziadek, too!"

Ursula's face fell. Victor held her hands in his. "We'll be here all week, Babcia! Lots of time to visit. You'll be sick of us by the time we leave!" he teased.

Ursula pushed at his arm. "Ve never tire of you, Victor. Eh, Tomasz?"

Tomasz shook his head and put his arm around Victor's shoulders giving him a hard squeeze.

As he looked at his grandparents, Victor thought how old and tired they looked. Ursula, a short stout woman was sixty-eight years old now. Her gray hair hung down her back in a tight braid. During the day she wore it in a braided coronet on top of her head. Tomasz was a tall gaunt man with a face like wrinkled brown paper, weathered by the rain and cold and a lifetime of working in the open air. He had the patient look of a man who had suffered many hardships and had accepted them all as part of life.

"Go to bed folks," Victor said. "We'll see you in the morning. Good night, Babcia, Dziadek." He kissed his grandmother on her cheek and picked up their bags from the hall floor. He started up the stairs, Renee following. She turned and looked down. "Good night, then!" she called out. She wasn't sure what she should call them.

Downstairs Tomasz turned out the lights and he and Ursula climbed up the stairs.

Ursula lay in bed beside Tomasz, who was already snoring. She felt uneasy. The confidence she had in herself and her uncomplicated life with her husband of fifty years was shaken by Renee's presence. The pretty young woman was from a different world. She didn't speak their language. And Victor seemed changed, too. Ursula could see he belonged more to Renee's world than to them and the farm where he'd grown up. During the years when his father, Walter, had been away at war, Victor and his mother had lived on the farm with his grandparents. They'd remained a tightly knit little family. But Renee was Victor's concern now. Ursula knew she would have to let go but she didn't want to. Victor and Tomasz were her whole life. She was fearful of losing her grandson.

"Ah, well! He's a man now," she sighed. She turned over and went to sleep.

~~

Victor closed their bedroom door. Renee was sitting on the bed.

"I wonder how they really feel about us being married," she said. They'd made a quick decision to marry because they wanted to stop at the farm on their way to Vancouver for a holiday with Renee's parents. The ceremony at the Justice of the Peace was just a formality. They'd been living together for over a year. Victor often joked to her that just living together was more fun than being married. The only guests at their wedding were a handful of friends from their workplaces. Victor's father had been killed in the Second World War when Victor was very young. His mother had died last year in Toronto.

Renee suspected Victor's grandparents didn't consider them married at all. Evidence of their strong Catholic faith was apparent throughout their home. Holy pictures of saints and gilt-edged icons were prominently displayed in every room. She grimaced as she wondered what they would think of her if they knew that she and Victor had lived together long before their marriage. She thought they'd blame her. She would be the object of their grandson living 'in sin.' She crawled into bed beside Victor and put her arms around him, seeking comfort.

The next morning Renee awakened alone. Her slim body was partly hidden under a thick feather comforter. She stretched her long legs. Her eyes blinked at the morning sun streaming through the window. She looked around the bedroom. She hadn't taken much notice of it the night before. It was a room caught in a time warp. It smelled of fresh wax. The oak dresser was old and ornately carved. It was draped with a white crocheted scarf, crisp with starch. A green glass tray with a few pins and buttons sat on top. It was chipped on one corner. A flowered curtain hung across the closet doorway. It was slightly parted in the middle, releasing the scent of mothballs. On the wall above the bed hung a picture of Christ, his heart exposed in flames. His liquid eyes stared out, fingers uplifted. Was it a blessing or an admonition, Renee wondered.

She reached for her sandals. She could hear voices in the kitchen. Ursula was shouting in Polish and she could hear Tomasz's muffled replies. She didn't know what they were saying but they seemed to be yelling at each other. She smiled as she remembered Victor joking, "There are two things a Polak knows how to do, and that's yell and slam doors."

She could hear Victor's voice. "Let her sleep, Babcia. It was a long drive and she's tired."

Ursula looked up fondly at her grandson towering over her. His smooth skin, prominent cheekbones and straight black hair were so like Tomasz when he was a young man. But their hands were different. Victor's were soft and white, his fingernails clean and trimmed. She smiled and shook her head. Thanks be to God he's never suffered like us, she thought.

The screen door slammed and Victor and his grandfather went out to the barn.

Ursula sat at the kitchen table with a basket piled high with wet clothes she'd just put through the wringer. Victor's idea of a hard journey amused her. A vivid picture of her long journey to Canada came to her. And how tired she was when she arrived.

Her thoughts were filled with the early years. She sighed remembering her two little boys lost to an epidemic of diphtheria that swept the community. The other two, Walter and Stanley, survived the disease, but less than a year later, four-year-old Stanley was playing at the creek behind the farm. He fell in and drowned. Walter, Victor's father, was the only one of their children to survive those early disasters, only to die later in the war.

There were times when the trauma of their children's deaths had almost driven them back to Poland, but they knew there was nothing for them there and they'd neither the will nor the money to go. And so, weighed down with grief, they worked quietly together in stoic acceptance of what they saw as God's will.

In later years, Tomasz had built a larger house with two bedrooms on the second floor replacing Stanley's earlier little log house that was now home to a flock of chickens.

Ursula could hear Renee moving about upstairs. Enough of this daydreaming, she said to herself and continued on with the washing.

Up in the bedroom, Renee pulled on a pair of jeans and a T-shirt. She filled a white china basin with water from a jug on the washstand and splashed the cold water on her face. The house didn't possess inside plumbing. Renee wished she could take her morning shower.

Downstairs Ursula bent down to pick up the basket of wet clothes to hang on the clothesline outside. Little tendrils of gray hair had sprouted over her ears. She wiped away the perspiration from her face with a corner of her apron. Ursula's Monday morning ritual wouldn't be interrupted for anything or anyone.

The kitchen was a pleasant room, the homey kind you would expect to find in a farmhouse. Ursula had painted the walls in a soft green with white trim. Pink geraniums grew in pots on the windowsill, adding a pleasant touch of colour to the room. Crisscross curtains, starched to wafer stiffness, hung at the double windows.

The night before, Tomasz had brought in pails of water from the pump in the yard and heated them this morning on the cookstove. Victor had wanted to buy his grandmother an automatic washer and dryer for Christmas after they'd put in electricity last year, but Ursula hadn't let him.

"I'm not dead yet, Victor," she laughed. "Save your money, Dziecko." Victor was convinced she didn't want the modern equipment because neither she nor his grandfather could understand the instructions and were too embarrassed to say so.

Ursula turned back from the kitchen doorway when Renee came into the room. The smell of bleach was so strong Renee gagged. Clouds of steam rose from the old washer groaning under the weight of its contents. Its clanking noises filled the kitchen. Ursula looked up.

"Good morning, Renee," she shouted above the clatter.

"Good morning Mrs. Krasinski." Renee replied. "Where is everyone this morning?"

"Victor with Dziadek in barn." Ursula motioned with her head. "Very busy!" she added with a laugh. "You go to milk cow?" She nodded at Renee's jeans. Her tone was one of gentle teasing. Renee didn't know how to react to her. She didn't want to get off on the wrong foot with Ursula so she said nothing.

"Coffee on stove!" Ursula shouted. "I make you breakfast." She wiped her hands on her apron.

"Oh, no thank-you." Renee raised her voice. "I never eat breakfast. I'll have some coffee, though." She helped herself from the blue enamel pot on the stove.

"You so skinny," Ursula said. "You need fatten up. Victor skinny, too. He should eat better or he get sick. He always eat good here with us."

Renee grimaced. She was anxious to get away from the kitchen and away from Ursula before she might say something she would regret. She felt a growing tension between them that she couldn't understand.

"I'll take some coffee to Vic," she said. She pushed open the screen door balancing the two cups in her hands.

Ursula looked after her in astonishment. "Nobody takes coffee to barn! Is dirty in der! Tomasz don't like dat!"

Renee ignored her and headed toward the barn. "This is not going well," she muttered.

Ursula shook her head and picked up the basket of wet clothes. She hung some on the clothesline outside and the rest she spread on the grass to dry in the sun. Fetching a pot from the kitchen she went to her garden to pick some vegetables for their lunch. Little barbs of jealousy began to pick at her. Renee's life seemed so easy.

At noon Renee and Victor came in. Tomasz followed them, wiping his shoes on the doormat. The table was set with heaping platters of potatoes, pork hocks and a variety of vegetables. Thick slices of homemade bread were piled on a plate. The chocolate tort they hadn't eaten last night sat on the sideboard for their dessert.

Renee wasn't in the habit of eating such a big lunch. Grabbing a sandwich and coffee was all she could manage in her lunch hour at work. Ursula kept pushing food at her. Renee didn't know how to react. She wanted to get along with her, but Ursula's abruptness kept her on the defensive. She didn't understand that because of her poor language skills the old woman couldn't express herself in the way she wanted and everything came out sounding like criticisms.

Ursula wanted Renee to like her too, but she couldn't understand the growing coldness between them. She watched as Renee picked at her food. Why isn't she eating? she wondered. Doesn't she like my cooking? It's good! Victor and Tomasz are eating everything.

After lunch, Victor showed Renee around the farm. They went down to the creek where as a child he used to wade and catch tadpoles in jars and keep them until they turned into frogs. Then he'd let them back into the creek.

"This is the creek where my Uncle Stanley drowned when he was just a little kid." Victor said. He looked off in the distance thinking about the other two children who'd died. "I often wonder what it would be like to have all those uncles." Renee knew that his father had died in the war. She was beginning to understand the reason for his deep affection for his grandparents.

As they sat on the grass beside the creek, Victor talked about his life on the farm with his grandparents and mother after his father went away to war. He was very young then. He told her how hard it was to be without his father although he loved his grandparents very much. He told her stories about their life in the old country that had fascinated him when he was a little boy. He tried to make Renee understand their old country attitudes and their feelings of uncertainty about her. He'd sensed the growing distance between her and his grandmother.

"It isn't that they don't like you, honey," he said. "But you're different. They're different. Nobody can change that. They mean well, but they have always lived on this farm and kept pretty much to themselves. They're a little suspicious of outsiders. They may seem gruff to you, but it is only because they can't express themselves the way they would like to. Can you imagine the frustration they must feel about that?"

"Maybe I've been too quick to judge. I've never known anyone quite like them. They really are wonderful people. But, as you say, they are different."

Victor's love for his grandparents stirred her deeply. She was already planning a strategy to narrow the gap between Ursula and herself.

It was late afternoon when the young couple returned to the farmhouse. Ursula was bustling about the kitchen. Renee had a sinking feeling when she saw all the food she was preparing, but she promised herself she would eat everything without protest. She understood now that Ursula's insistence was her way of showing her hospitality.

"I'll do that, Mrs. Krasinski," she said, taking a bowl of green beans from Ursula. "You've been working all day. I could have picked them for you, too, if Vic and I hadn't been so long at the creek."

"Is OK, Renee. I do potatoes."

The two women sat together intent on preparing the vegetables for supper. Ursula was silent. Renee was thinking this was a good chance to get to know her better.

"I've really enjoyed meeting you and Mr. Krasinski. Vic's told me so much about you. I hope we can come again before too long."

"Tak, tak!" Ursula nodded her head eagerly.

"I grew up in the city and this is the first time I've been on a farm," Renee went on as she trimmed the beans. "It's so quiet and peaceful here compared to Toronto. I know Vic looks forward to coming here and seeing you both. It's been a real treat for me, too! I hope we can come back soon."

Ursula looked up. "You comin' anytime, Renee. Ve always glad to see Victor and now you." She smiled at Renee. "He pick good wife," she added shyly.

Tomasz and Victor came in after washing up at the pump outside. Renee had set the table and they all sat down to eat. Tomasz took his usual place at the head of the table. Victor and Renee sat across from each other. Ursula sat at the other end when she wasn't jumping up to wait on them.

Tomasz bowed his head and said grace in Polish. When he finished he and Ursula made the sign of the cross and she began passing the dishes. First to come was the chicken soup, steaming hot and thick with homemade noodles and little chunks of potatoes, carrots, and cauliflower all mingling together in the spicy broth. The silence was broken by Tomasz blowing on his soup. Victor winked at Renee.

She looked at Ursula exclaiming, "I've never tasted such delicious soup!" Ursula beamed as she gathered up the empty bowls, refusing Renee's offer to help.

"Sit," she ordered. "Kitchen too small for two!" She bustled around the room setting more platters and bowls of steaming food on the table. A crisp roasted chicken with fragrant dressing was placed before Tomasz for carving. Steam wafted up from the bowls of vegetables and thick brown gravy. Homemade bread and butter were set on the table.

Renee groaned silently when Ursula announced that she'd made a banana cream pie especially for Victor. "He always like dat pie," she said, laughing.

When most of the food had disappeared, the dishes were cleared and mammoth wedges of pie were set in front of everyone. There was no denying that it was delicious. As she swallowed the last forkful Renee felt as if she would burst.

They teased Victor who was shoveling a second helping of bananas and custard into his mouth.

"Oy, oy, oy, Victor! Slow down." Tomasz was grinning at him.

"You haven't lost your touch, Babcia!" Victor exclaimed, his mouth full. "Fantastic dinner," he said, smiling at his grandmother. "What do you think, Renee?"

Renee looked at Ursula. "You can tell I don't have it in the cooking department!" she said with a grin.

"You come back! I show you!" Ursula said. "You help me talk good. I help you cook good!" They all laughed at what seemed to be a sensible offer.

The talk had turned to children. Tomasz was anxious to become a great-grandfather. "You have baby soon?" He looked at Renee. She was taken by surprise by his direct question. She looked at Victor for help.

Victor, his eyes twinkling, patted Tomasz on his shoulder.

"Soon, Dziadek, soon!" he laughed. "Be patient! I promise we'll name him Tomasz after you," he added. Renee grinned and nodded in agreement. A smile of pleasure spread over the old man's face.

For the first time, Ursula joined the conversation. Shyly at first, she remarked on how lucky Renee was to have everything when the time came for her to have a child.

"When I vas young, babies just come. Every year! I don' know anyting dat time. I so scare I run to cornfield and cry for Matka. Poor Tomasz! He don't know what to do for me." She laughed as she told it.

"When first baby comin', is vinter. Snow start to fall and vind come up. It vas blizzard outside. Big snows cover kitchen vindow. Tomasz not even go to barn to feed animals. Doctor not comin'. Neighbour farm too far. Tomasz don't see nuttink outside. When baby come, he roll up sleeves. He's young man. He only know about animals on farm. But he bring baby out. He very good for me and baby." She reached out and squeezed his arm. "He sleep in chair by bed all night. Baby and I sleep. In morning he bring me bread and coffee. Then Tomasz go for doctor. He put the snowshoes and valk to Tamarack. It vas beautiful day. Sun shining like new penny."

She remembered the old country doctor coming with his horse and cutter and Tomasz sitting beside him. She went on with her story.

"When doctor check up me and baby, he say to Tomasz, 'Good job, Tomasz. I don't do better myself!' Remember, Dziadek?" Ursula looked lovingly at her husband. Tomasz hung his head modestly.

Everyone was quiet for a few moments. The faces of Ursula's dead children, her parents in Poland, and her old friend, Stanley, filled the room and her voice faded down to a whisper.

Renee looked at the old couple and slowly shook her head. Now she understood why Ursula had seemed so distant. Why, she's afraid of losing Vic, the only living child left of her little family. Renee got up from the table and put her arms around Ursula, breaking the silence.

"I may be Vic's wife," she spoke quietly. "But you and Tomasz will always be his loving family. You're a remarkable woman, Babcia," she said. "I hope you don't mind me calling you Babcia?" she asked. She kissed the old woman on the cheek and Ursula didn't mind at all. The two women shared the common bond of womanhood, and the hardships and frustrations of two different worlds melded together.

Bitter Herbs

Ugh! That awful stink again! Disinfectant. The perfume of nursing homes. And that smell of decaying bodies and the ever-present stench of urine. I hate it! And I hate this place too! Everywhere I look there's a jumble of wheelchairs and walkers and old people shuffling down the hallways. It isn't safe to go outside your door! I shouldn't be here. I'm not one of these people! I came here only because my nieces tricked me with their promise. "Oh, you'll love it Auntie Mel," they said. They just packed me off and out of sight like an old horse to the glue factory. My sister Beth's girls. I always thought they liked me. They call me Auntie Mel to my face, as if they really care. But I've heard them snickering behind my back and calling me "Mel from Hell." I may be old, but by Heaven, I still have all my marbles! And I'm a lot more caring than those two with their stringy hair and skirts up to their armpits, wagging their flat bums in my face. And after all I've done for them! I never liked either of them much anyway. You'd wonder how they ever belonged to Beth. Beth would never treat me like that if she were still alive.

And another thing. Why wasn't I allowed to bring my own furniture - my lovely carved oak dresser and bed? Of all the falderal! I've never heard the likes of it! Those two little schemers sold everything I owned without even a by-your-leave! But I still have a few trinkets with me, remnants of better times. I'll throw them all in the trash before those two get any of them. Even my little opal pendant. The one Mother gave me on my tenth birthday.

That was around the time I went on the train to Rumbling Rapids to visit Aunt Sarah and Uncle Jack and my goofy cousin, Freddy. I never bothered much with his brothers. They were older. I think Freddy was my age, ten, or maybe he was eleven, I'm not really sure any more. We had good times together. I can't believe he died last year. Seventy-six, he was. Who's next? Me? God forbid! I'm not ready to meet my Maker.

Beth and I always got along pretty well, for sisters. Too bad that she took sick with a cold just before we were to take that trip. Mother wanted me to wait until she was better, but no, I went without her. I can still see Beth lying in bed asleep and me tip-toeing past her room. I was wearing her new dress. She said I couldn't have it, but I sneaked it out of her closet when she was asleep. It looked better on me anyway. It should've been mine. When she found out she was so mad at me she wouldn't speak to me for a long time. But she got over it. Now that I think of it, I feel a little regret about it all. Oh! Beth! I wish I'd waited for you.

Oh! I remember now! The day I went to Rumbling Rapids on the train. Alone. Mother was shouting orders at the conductor while I stood dreaming. I was wishing she'd stop her yelling and go home. She was spoiling everything.

She always liked to put a damper on my make-believe. Said it was silly and I was too old for all that nonsense. So I jumped on board, without even saying good-bye. I sat down and pretended to be a rich Victorian lady married to a major in the army. No, he must have been a colonel! I never would've settled for anything less. I was travelling to meet him in Paris, or was it India? I forget which. I was in my own little world. A waiter handed me a glass of sherry on a silver tray and called me "Ma'am." No, it was only the conductor shouting, "Tickets! Tickets! Tickets, please!"

I always loved going to Rumbling Rapids. I had to travel by train and boat. It was years before they got around to putting in a road. That's the government for you! Sitting on their hands, spending our tax money willy-nilly on who-knows-what.

I can still hear the thundering water cascading down the cement chute at the power plant. And that deafening boom when it hits the bottom and empties into the river. You could get used to that noise living there, I suppose. Sometimes at night it was like a lullaby. Sometimes it kept me awake.

Old Uncle Jack, he's gone now. He kept the marine railway running. Music to his ears, he used to say. That grinding and clanking of winches hauling the boats over the fall in the river. He had stories to tell that would split your sides. He was a corker all right!

I remember as clear as day when we learned to swim in the canoe slip. Uncle Jack tied thick ropes around our waists and Beth and I jumped right in. Fearless, we were. Fearless water babies, the both of us! The water was over our heads. Uncle Jack would stand on the cement skirt above holding the ropes and shouting, "Move your feet! Paddle like a dog!"

Then there was that time when Beth and I got off the train wearing white nail polish. It was all the go then. Uncle Jack took one look and ordered us to take it off. "Tout suite," he'd said. We didn't know what that meant but we'd picked and scraped it off as best we could.

Beth's in my mind today. And her wretched life with her husband, Bert. That old devil. I always thought he'd killed her! Oh, yes, it was cancer all right, but she'd been dead inside for years. Bert might as well have put a gun to her head and pulled the trigger. And all those kids! What was she thinking of? Too bad the doctor's snip-and-stitch at his birth didn't go up a little higher. It would have solved that problem once and for all! I knew the marriage wouldn't work out. But you couldn't tell her. She wanted him and that was that! Later on, she knew she'd made a terrible mistake, but she wouldn't talk about it. He was good looking, I'll give him that. A finely chiseled face, boyish looking with a head of thick black hair curling around his neck.

I wonder what became of him. He turns up in my dreams sometimes, although I don't know why. A dirty old bum riding atop a box-car. It was the only way out of town for poor people in those Depression days. And Bert wanted out! Oh, yes! He could be one of the many poor drifters crushed to death while trying to leap on a moving freight train. The drunken old fool might have chucked himself under the wheels. Maybe lying there between the rails, his legs severed and bloody beside him. There was no work anywhere. Not that he was looking for any. All he ever looked for was another skirt to chase or another bottle of booze. Well, good riddance, that's what I say. He was a waste of space anyway.

I can't keep my eyes open. Drifting...drifting... Who's that whispering? God Almighty! Is that you Beth? Don't be angry! I'm sorry! I'm sorry! I should've waited for you to come with me on the train. Forgive me!

No! no! Wake up you silly old fool! It's not Beth. Beth died years ago. It's Margaret, the "Mother Superior" of the nursing home. Here she comes. Rumbling into my room like a freight train, her big caboose swaying in the breeze! Don't bump into my lamp and break it, you clumsy ox!

"Would you like some tea or juice, Mrs. MacGregor?" Her loud voice booms across the room. It sets my teeth on edge. We're not all deaf just because we're old, you know!

"Just the tea, thanks, Margaret." I say it softly to keep from screaming at her. In the cup this time, fatso, instead of in the saucer.

"There you are, dear."

Lord love us! There's that condescending tone again! I hate that! You'd think I was ten years old. One of these days I'll tell her how insulting it is. But not now! Why on earth does she wear those squeaky shoes! And just look at those jumbo hips writhing under her uniform. Disgusting! Clink, clink. And you'd think she could keep the juice glasses and teapots from rattling. Just put some space between them, for God's sake. Hallelujah! She's leaving now. Good-bye Mrs. Bugger!

Oh, my Lord! Is that really me in the mirror over there? I look so old. What's happened to my face? It looks like crinkled up paper. My eyes are so heavy-lidded staring back at me. And so hollow. Is it a death mask? I can't look. Drink your tea while it's hot. That's the only good thing I can say about this place. They make good tea, and it's always hot. It makes me think of when I had tea in the parlour at home when mother's friends came to call. I always wanted to stay and listen to their gossip, but they would send me packing after I finished my tea and cake. Oh, the stories they would tell! They didn't know I was out in the hall listening to every word. I was so young then, and believed everything. It was old Mrs. McPhee's prattle that kept my ears glued to the door. Gory details of the horrors of childbirth. She scared me half to death! I remember thinking I sure wouldn't go through anything like that! And I never did!

Maybe Robert and I should've had children. I could've had my own daughters caring for me instead of those two schemers of Beth's.

I can still hear the gales of laughter and Mrs. McPhee describing the enemas she'd had after her son was born.

"They rammed the butt end of the tube up to my follicles! Like a plumber clearing a clogged pipe," she'd cackle. And she'd squeeze her knees together as if to prevent any further invasions. My knees are pressed together now with the thought of it. She was a pip all right, old Mrs. McPhee!

It was boring on the train that day without Beth. Nothing to look at out of the window. No trees, no flowers. Just rocks and boulders and scrubby bushes. Looked like the surface of the moon.

I can still hear the conductor's shouts as he swung down the aisle. "Next stop, Rumbling Rapids!" He always stopped at our seat. He knew Beth and me. We'd taken this trip so often.

That train always jolted you out of your seat as it jerked to a stop. I had to stand up on the seat to get my suitcase down. No one offered to help. Freddy was supposed to meet me. I stood on the train steps like a scared kitten. Where was he? The platform was deserted except for the three Morley brothers skulking around. I was always afraid of them. They were all half-witted, no mistaking it.

The oldest, Tom, was sixteen. Next was George. The youngest, Billy, was the one I remember best because he always came up to me. He was about fourteen. Three of them! All born a year apart and none of them had anything above the collar button! I often wondered did their parents just keep trying, hoping someday they'd get it right? A person ought to know when to call it quits!

Aunt Sarah always told us not to be afraid of them.

"They wouldn't hurt a flea!" she'd say. Well, maybe and maybe not.

There I was with the train puffing out of sight and me all alone except for those three pairs of vacant eyes targeting me. Then Billy started walking slowly toward me. His brothers held back, fidgeting and twitching. Billy got so close to me I could see the drool dribbling down his knobby chin. I backed away. George shrieked with laughter, coughing and choking, bits of saliva flying from his mouth. Tom just stood there scratching his crotch. I didn't dare breathe. I thought I'd faint right there and then. What would they have done then? Freddy! Where were you? Then I'd hear a snicker from behind the tool shed.

"Freddy! Is that you?" He'd stumble out, red-faced and laughing. I wanted to kill him.

"They ain't goin' to hurt you, Melissa," he'd say. There were times when I hated him. Always playing tricks on people.

"Hi, gang! How're ya' all doin' today?" Freddy would call to the brothers who were lined up like three monuments to lunacy.

They liked my cousin. Their faces would light up when he talked to them. But I'd drag him away.

"See ya, guys!" he'd yell. Three heads bobbed up and down.

"Wave at them or something," he'd growl in my ear. But I could only lift a limp hand. I often wonder what became of them after their parents died. Locked up somewhere, I suppose.

What's that tapping sound? "Who's there? Freddy? Is that you?" No, no, no! It's Margaret again.

"Well, Margaret, what do you want now?"

"Don't snarl, Mrs. MacGregor. I just want to see if you're all right."

"I'm fine! What do you think! I don't want anything so leave me alone!" I wish she'd quit that infernal grinning and that red face so close to me. She smells like bleach. And look at her waddle.

"I'm leaving now, but I'll be back."

"Please! Do me a favour and don't bother! Here! Take my empty cup and saucer." Those red, beefy hands!

They look ridiculous. Like a bear holding a rose. You'd think she'd take better care of her hands. Put some lotion on them or something.

Oh, my Lord! They aren't Margaret's hands at all. They're small and soft like Beth's. They ARE Beth's hands! There's her wedding ring. That small cheap band Bert gave her. Oh, Beth, it's so good to see you. You look so young and so happy! No! Don't go! Take my hand, Beth. I'm coming with you!

ISBN 141201902-8